3 3121 00080 0438

J F Bryant, Bonnie S124 V. 77
Bryant, Bonnie.
Rocking horse WITHDRAWN FROM
Dickinson Public Library
(The Saddle Club #77)

AS GOO[...]

Carole grabbed Ste[...] their tack room bef[...] Veronica. "Not a w[...] Meg, or Betsy, for the rest of the weekend, from any of us. I was never so embarrassed, Stevie. Max shouldn't have had to talk to us like that."

Stevie hung her head. She sat down on their tack trunk and looked up at Carole. "I know," she said. "But this is going to be an awful day. There are too many coops out there. Belle's going to be eliminated, and then we won't even get a team score."

"She'll be fine," Lisa said, sitting down next to Stevie. "Remember how much she loves you. She'll jump anything if she thinks she's jumping it for you."

"I just don't have the guts," Stevie said. "I look at those jumps and I think, *Wow, that's big*, and as soon as I've thought *that*, I'm as good as finished."

D0019189

Other Skylark Books you will enjoy
Ask your bookseller for the books you have missed

THE WINNING STROKE (American Gold Swimmers #1)
by Sharon Dennis Wyeth

COMPETITION FEVER (American Gold Gymnasts #1)
by Gabrielle Charbonnet

THE GREAT DAD DISASTER *by Betsy Haynes*

THE GREAT MOM SWAP *by Betsy Haynes*

BREAKING THE ICE (Silver Blades #1) *by Melissa Lowell*

SAVE THE UNICORNS (Unicorn Club #1) *by Francine Pascal*

THE SADDLE CLUB

ROCKING HORSE

BONNIE BRYANT

DICKINSON AREA PUBLIC
LIBRARY
139 Third Street West
Dickinson, North Dakota 58601

A SKYLARK BOOK
NEW YORK • TORONTO • LONDON • SYDNEY • AUCKLAND

RL 5, 009–012

ROCKING HORSE

A Bantam Skylark Book / May 1998

Skylark Books is a registered trademark of Bantam Books, a division of
Bantam Doubleday Dell Publishing Group, Inc. Registered in U.S. Patent
and Trademark Office and elsewhere.

"The Saddle Club" is a registered trademark of Bonnie Bryant Hiller.
The Saddle Club design/logo, which consists of a riding crop and a riding
hat, is a trademark of Bantam Books.

"USPC" and "Pony Club" are registered trademarks of The United States
Pony Clubs, Inc., at The Kentucky Horse Park, 4071 Iron Works Pike,
Lexington, KY 40511-8462.

All rights reserved.
Copyright © 1998 by Bonnie Bryant Hiller.
Cover art © 1998 by Paul Casale.
No part of this book may be reproduced or transmitted in any form or by any
means, electronic or mechanical, including photocopying, recording, or by
any information storage and retrieval system, without permission in writing
from the publisher.
For information address: Bantam Books.

If you purchased this book without a cover you should be aware that this
book is stolen property. It was reported as "unsold and destroyed" to the
publisher, and neither the author nor the publisher has received any pay-
ment for this "stripped book."

ISBN 0-553-48627-6

Published simultaneously in the United States and Canada.

Bantam Books are published by Bantam Books, a division of Bantam Doubleday
Dell Publishing Group, Inc. Its trademark, consisting of the words "Bantam
Books" and the portrayal of a rooster, is Registered in U.S. Patent and Trade-
mark Office and in other countries. Marca Registrada. Bantam Books, 1540
Broadway, New York, New York 10036.

PRINTED IN THE UNITED STATES OF AMERICA

OPM   0 9 8 7 6 5 4 3 2 1

*I would like to express my special thanks
to Kimberly Brubaker Bradley for her help
in the writing of this book.*

CAROLE HANSON STARTED counting out loud when the log jump was five strides away. It was something Max, her instructor, insisted on so that she could learn to ride in a rhythm to each jump. "Five, four, three, two, one!" she chanted. *Blastoff!* she thought as her bay gelding, Starlight, lifted them both into the air.

Starlight's grace and power always gave her a thrill. As soon as he landed, Carole looked for their next jump, a low stone wall. She turned and counted off the strides, and Starlight jumped it, just as well as he had jumped the log pile. Just as well, in fact, as he'd jumped the entire course. Carole pulled him up

1

and patted him, her face aglow. She loved riding outdoors over solid cross-country fences.

"Nice job!" Max said. "Next time, go a little deeper into the corner before the rolltop. On Saturday's cross-country course you'll have all the room you need, and you always want to try to give Starlight a straight line to the fences."

Carole nodded. No matter how well she and Starlight did, they could always do better. It was one of the things she liked most about riding. Carole's goals were to be one of the best riders in the world and to learn everything possible about horses and riding.

"Meg, same course," Max said. Meg Durham asked Barq, the horse she was riding, to pick up a canter, and they started for the first fence. Max turned his attention to her. Carole rode over to her two best friends, Lisa Atwood and Stevie Lake, who were waiting their turns to jump at the side of the field.

"Fantastic!" Lisa said. "You guys were in perfect harmony—much better than Prancer and me on our first try." She unconsciously stroked the neck of the mare she was riding, a lesson horse named Prancer. She longed for a horse of her own, but she loved Prancer very much. Harmony, however, was not always one of the strong points of their relationship. Lisa was studious and quiet; Prancer was flighty and skittish. Over the jumping course she'd bucked three times. If Prancer were a person, Lisa often thought, she'd be a three-year-old girl, prone to temper tantrums and fond of frilly dresses. Fortunately, Prancer was a horse.

"If you keep riding like that," said Stevie, "and Lisa can hold Prancer together—you coped with her really well, Lisa, even though she did buck—and if there aren't any coop jumps on the course on Saturday—"

"Don't count your chickens," Lisa advised, at the same time as Carole said, "You're psyching yourself out of coop jumps. Stop it." All three of them laughed. They understood each other very well—so well, in fact, that they had formed a club called The Saddle Club. Its only two rules were that members had to be horse-crazy and that they had to be willing to help one another out.

"Quiet over there," Max ordered, looking toward the group. The girls instantly quieted. They loved Max, who ran Pine Hollow with a firm hand, and they knew perfectly well that they were not supposed to be talking during one of his lessons.

"But there's so much to talk about!" Stevie whispered. Carole and Lisa nodded understandingly. It was finally spring, warm and pleasant. The horses had shed their winter coats and were full of spring vigor. That vigor would soon be put to good use: On

Friday, they were all leaving for a weekend-long Regional Pony Club cross-country rally, where Stevie, Carole, and Lisa would compete as a team.

On course, Meg approached the final jump with Barq, who was another of Max's lesson horses. Barq apparently didn't like the look of the stone wall, because as Meg turned him toward it, he tried to keep turning and run past the jump. Meg corrected him quickly and pressed him forward. Barq jumped it a little awkwardly, but he did jump it—and in a cross-country competition that was all that counted.

"Nice job, Meg!" Carole called out, despite Max's rule. She knew Max wouldn't mind this time—and Meg had done well. Carole had ridden Barq quite a bit before she had gotten Starlight, and she knew he could be difficult sometimes.

"Yes," Max said, with a half grin in Carole's direction. "Very well done, Meg. Remember to keep your head about you like that on Saturday. Barq will jump anything if you're confident enough about telling him to. Who's next? Veronica, go ahead."

"The same course, Max? Or should I try something a little more difficult?" A black-haired rider named Veronica diAngelo trotted toward Max. Her elegant gray Thoroughbred, Danny, curved his neck against the bit. "I do like Danny to feel he's been *slightly* challenged."

With difficulty, Stevie stifled a groan. She hated Veronica so much! It wasn't just that Veronica was rich enough to buy the most expensive, perfect horse Stevie had ever seen, and the most expensive, elegant riding gear. It wasn't just that she had a talent for making all the other riders feel shabby and insignificant. It was, Stevie decided, that she didn't seem to care about anything except proving that she was the most important person around.

At Pine Hollow, all the riders were expected to help care for their horses and to do extra work around the stable. Veronica never lifted a well-manicured finger to help. Why Max tolerated her was something Stevie never fully understood. She didn't think it was just because of Veronica's money or her family's social position. Lisa had once said that she thought Max wanted to reform Veronica— that he thought if he worked with her long enough, she might actually start to care about the horses she rode. Lisa thought that might take decades; Stevie was sure it would take much longer than that.

"Let's stick with this course," Max said rather sternly. "Remember, even Danny can't be perfect unless you give him the chance. You've got to pay attention and ride him well."

Veronica nodded, suddenly serious. She was a good rider—that was the worst of it. She was tough competition, and she, Meg, and Betsy would be one of the teams up against The Saddle Club this weekend.

" '*Even* Danny'?" Stevie whispered angrily. "I can't believe Max would phrase it like that! Danny's not *that* good!" She patted her mare's neck defensively. Belle was a mixed-breed horse, half Saddlebred and half Arabian. She was sweet and wonderful and Stevie loved her, but she never floated across the ground with anything like Danny's well-bred grace.

"Yes, he *is*," Carole said as Veronica and Danny took the first fence. "He's the best horse I've seen since Southwood." Southwood had gone to the Olympics.

Lisa agreed with Carole. Danny really was that good—and it was a rotten shame that he had a jerk like Veronica as an owner. Max and Red, Pine Hollow's groom, made sure that Danny was always well cared for. But Lisa thought Danny should have been loved, too.

"Well, it doesn't matter," Stevie said bitterly. "Veronica might finish at the top of every class, but her *team* won't necessarily be unbeatable. They're going to combine everyone's scores, you know."

"I know," Carole said. "And winning isn't everything. If we all do our best, I'll be more than happy."

"So will I," Stevie said, "provided our best includes beating Veronica—and Phil. Just kidding," she added hastily when her friends frowned. Phil Marsten, Stevie's boyfriend, rode with another Pony Club. He and his friends A.J. and Bart would also be a team at the rally. Stevie could get very competitive, and in the past she had nearly broken up with Phil because of it.

"I'm kidding about Phil," she said, "but not about Veronica. I want to blow her team off the map."

"Fortunately," Lisa said as she watched Veronica take the last fence just as well as she'd taken the first, "it's not all jumping. It's not even all riding."

"No. And I think Miss Perfect might have a little trouble with the horse care and stable management," said Stevie.

"We can only hope," Carole added with a wry grin. She didn't worry much about winning, it was true, as long as she and Starlight did their best and learned from the experience. But she did want to best Veronica. It always bothered her how little Veronica seemed to care about her horse.

"We'll be great," Stevie said emphatically. She wished she felt as sure as she sounded. Danny was so stupendous, and Stevie had had some trouble with Belle lately. They just couldn't jump coop jumps.

"Betsy's going to take Coconut," Lisa reported. "I heard her ask Max if she could." Like Prancer, Coconut was a lesson horse. Betsy rode well, and Lisa knew they weren't going to be easy to beat. She just hoped Prancer didn't act crazy at the rally.

"Quiet over there!" Max reminded them again. He spoke to Veronica about her ride, then sent Adam out on the course.

"And the week after the rally, there's the dance!" Stevie whispered. "I can't wait for that, either!"

"It's not your dance," Lisa whispered back teasingly. "What if you don't get invited?" Willow Creek Junior High was hosting a big spring dance, outdoors, under a giant tent on the football field. Lisa and Carole both went to school there, but Stevie—and Veronica—went to Fenton Hall, a nearby private school.

"Of course I'm invited," Stevie said a little indignantly. "Lisa, how could you forget? I'm your date, and Phil is Carole's."

Lisa laughed. "That's right." It was an open dance, which meant that the students could invite anyone they chose.

"After all, it's not like we have other dates," Carole said. "There isn't any boy that I even half want to invite—right, Lisa?"

"Uh, right," Lisa said. She adjusted the strap on her riding helmet to hide the fact that she was blushing a bit. In fact, there *was* a boy Lisa at least half wanted to invite—Phil's friend Bart. He was very quiet, and Lisa didn't know him that well, but she was quiet too so they probably would be a good match. Bart was tall and cute, and he certainly rode well. So far Lisa hadn't had the guts to admit her feelings to her friends. They weren't very strong feelings, after all.

But why not invite him? Lisa argued with herself. *The worst he can do is say no.*

And if he says no I'll just die, she admitted. Plus, how could she ever get up the nerve to ask Bart when she couldn't even talk about him to her two best friends?

"Stevie, come ahead," Max said. Stevie clucked to Belle encouragingly and they started out. The first three fences went fine, but the fourth was a coop. Coops were double-paneled fences often used in hunt country to cover part of a wire fence and make it jumpable. To Stevie, jumping a coop was like jumping an A-frame house sideways: It looked huge. Stevie Lake didn't like to admit she was afraid of anything, but coops really bothered her.

She knew Max's coop was not even three feet tall, shorter than many of the jumps in his field. She knew Belle could jump any three-foot obstacle with ease. But as Stevie turned the corner to the coop, she felt her own muscles tense. She held her breath and tried to make herself urge Belle forward while at the same time bracing herself for Belle to stop.

Across the field, Carole groaned. "C'mon, Stevie," she whispered. "You can do it."

"She's telling Belle to stop at the same time as she's telling her to jump," Lisa whispered. Stevie's legs were saying go forward, but her seat, shoulders, and hands were all saying whoa.

"I know," Carole said. "Guess which one Belle is going to pick?"

Sure enough, Belle slid to a halt right in front of the coop. "Stevie, that was your fault," Max said sternly.

"I know," Stevie said miserably. Belle wasn't truly afraid of coops—yet. But if Stevie convinced her that they were a problem, Belle might have a phobia for life. "I'm sorry, darling," she whispered to her horse.

"Come again," Max said. "And mean it this time."

"Right." Stevie licked her lips and circled Belle toward the fence. She tried really hard to tell Belle to jump—but Belle stopped.

"Keep breathing," Max said patiently. "Look over the jump. Don't look at it. Just think about being on the other side."

This time Carole and Lisa could see that Stevie approached the jump much more confidently. But Belle had gotten into the habit of stopping in front of it, and she stopped again. Stevie tapped Belle en-

10

couragingly with her crop and tried again. Belle stopped again.

"Oh no," Lisa groaned. This was getting ugly. She felt so sorry for Stevie.

Suddenly Prancer's ears went flat as Veronica cantered Danny by without warning.

"We'll just give you a little lead," Veronica said in her most annoying syrupy voice. She clucked to Danny, who breezed past Belle and jumped the coop as effortlessly as though it were a pole laid on the ground.

"The nerve of her!" Carole grumbled. Veronica hadn't asked Max if she could help—she'd just butted in, as always.

Stevie held Belle in place with trembling hands. "Show-off!" she spit. She circled Belle, drove her heels into her flanks, and launched her over the coop. Belle cleared it easily.

"That's enough!" Max said. "Both of you know better. Veronica, when I want your help, I'll ask for it. Stevie, you know better than to lose your temper during a lesson. Take it again."

Stevie jumped the coop again, but already some of her bravado was gone. Belle started to refuse and then jumped at the last minute, tossing Stevie awkwardly back into the saddle. Stevie jumped the rest of the course with her mouth set in a straight line, and Carole and Lisa knew she wasn't over her problem with coops. Veronica had more likely been a hindrance than a help—which was probably, Lisa realized, exactly her intention.

When Stevie finished jumping, Max gave them all a lecture. "You know I expect the proper Pony Club spirit from all my riders, whether in lessons or in competition," he said. "That spirit includes cooperation, respect, and good sportsmanship. I'd better see it in action this weekend."

"Yes, Max," they chorused.

"As long as Miss Goody Two-shoes can be a good sport about losing," Stevie muttered. From the look on Max's face, she knew he had heard her. She didn't care.

" 'THREE STABLE SHEETS,' " Carole read from the list of equipment in her hand. It was Friday afternoon, and she, Lisa, and Stevie were making final preparations for the Pony Club rally.

"Check," Lisa said, putting the folded sheets into Carole's tack trunk. The Pony Club ran its events under very strict rules, and at rallies every team had to bring all its own equipment. If a team was found to be missing something important—a horse first aid kit, for example—it would be given penalty points.

"Next we need coolers, and then our saddles,"

Carole said. "Two can go in this trunk, and the other one can go in Stevie's. Where is Stevie, anyway?"

"She's helping Max get the ponies loaded," Meg called from across the tack room, where she and Betsy were packing their team's trunks. "Nickel was giving Jessica a hard time."

"Oh," Carole said understandingly. There were actually two rallies going on that weekend: one for younger, less experienced riders, and one for older riders such as The Saddle Club. Horse Wise, Pine Hollow's Pony Club, had two teams entered in each competition. Since Max's van could hold only eight horses, he was taking the younger kids and their ponies to the show grounds first, then coming back for The Saddle Club, Meg, Betsy, Veronica, and their horses.

"Here's your saddle," Lisa said, gently placing it in the trunk. "Do you have extra stirrup leathers?"

"Sure." Carole's brow creased in concentration. "Where did I put them?" She lifted the lid of the trunk they'd already packed and peered inside.

"Hey," Stevie called to them as she came into the room. "The little kids are on their way, and Max will be back in forty-five minutes for us. We should be ready, he says."

"Has anyone seen my lucky crop?" Veronica strolled into the tack room, elegantly dressed as always. She didn't look ready for a weekend rally. Ve-

14

ronica gave The Saddle Club a disdainful glance as she walked over to Meg and Betsy. "I thought I put it near my new show coat. I just can't imagine going to a show without it—not, of course, that I'll need luck."

"No, of course not," Stevie said, her voice dripping with sarcasm.

Veronica ignored her. "Have you seen it, Meg dear?" she asked. "It's the one with the sterling silver top."

"Didn't you put it in your duffel bag?" Meg asked. "With all your other clothes?"

"Well—no. But maybe the maid packed it for me. I gave her explicit instructions. I'll go check."

"Grab that bridle hook from the office while you're out there, will you?" Betsy asked. "Max said we could borrow that one. Is Danny ready to go?"

"I'll ask Red," Veronica said as she disappeared.

"She'll ask Red?" Stevie asked in amazement. "Red knows if her horse is ready, but she doesn't?"

Lisa elbowed Stevie in the ribs to silence her. Even though Meg and Betsy were pretty nice, they had both been Veronica's friends for a long time. Stevie rolled her eyes but nodded. She took her saddle off its rack and tucked it into her tack trunk, then checked Carole's list and added some baling twine and a pair of scissors. They would need them to hang buckets and feed tubs in the horses' stalls.

15

Veronica came back in. "Good news!" she said. "My crop was in my suitcase! That silly maid tucked it in between my shirts, so I couldn't find it before."

"Silly maid," Lisa said, shaking her head. "It's so hard to find good help these days."

"That's great, Veronica," said Betsy. "Do you have the bridle hook?"

Veronica looked blank. "What bridle hook?"

"The one Max said we could use for the rally."

Veronica sighed. "I'm afraid I'm not exactly sure what you're talking about," she said. "If you'll excuse me, I need to make sure Red finished oiling my bits."

Betsy looked at Meg and shrugged. "I'll go get it," she said. Neither girl seemed to mind doing all Veronica's work.

"How could she not know what a bridle hook is?" Carole asked. "Even for Veronica, that's pretty obtuse." Bridle hooks looked like miniature anchors. They couldn't be mistaken for anything else around a stable.

"C'mon," Stevie said with a snort. "Bridle hooks are used for cleaning tack, and we all know Veronica's never done that in her entire life."

"With a horse like Danny," Meg said loftily, "she shouldn't have to." She shut her tack trunk with a click and walked out of the room.

"Poor Meg," Lisa said. "She and Betsy always stick

16

up for Veronica, but Veronica never even seems to notice."

"Meg chooses to do it," Carole said. "Nobody makes her."

"Well," said Stevie, checking Carole's list one last time before closing her trunk, "I'm sure she thinks that having Danny on her team is enough of an asset to make up for having Veronica. But unless Danny's learned to take the horse care test or set up and clean up his own stall, I'm not sure he'll make enough of a difference."

As in all combined training events, the rally would put every horse and rider through three different riding tests: dressage, cross-country jumping, and show jumping. Any mistake made in competition would cost the pair penalty points. Rallies differed from other competitions, though, in that they required the teams to be able to care for their horses as well. Once at the show grounds, each team would be wholly on its own. The Saddle Club couldn't ask Max for any help or advice except during their one official cross-country course walk. Adult inspectors could penalize them at any time for any infraction of the rules for horse care, tack care, organization, or cleanliness. The riders would also answer questions about different aspects of horse health.

Carole loved rallies. She loved being tested on everything she knew, and she loved being totally responsible for Starlight. Of course, if she or Starlight was injured or became sick, Max and the other officials would help her right away. But as long as they were still competing, they were on their own.

"We're a great team," Carole said. "That's the best thing about us and the worst thing about a person like Veronica. She won't even think to help Meg and Betsy. They'll end up carrying her all weekend."

"They can't lose too many points for horse care," Lisa said glumly. "Danny's in glorious condition, and I saw Veronica's tack before Meg put it in her trunk. Red must have been up half the night cleaning it. It looks great."

"And I'm sure Meg and Betsy will have time to clean Danny's stall," Stevie said.

"Oh well," Lisa said. "We'll have to do our best, like Carole always says. And we'd better get the horses ready. Max will be back soon."

They shoved the heavy trunks out to the aisle and went to their horses' stalls. The three had already groomed Belle, Prancer, and Starlight, and each horse wore a neat stable sheet to keep it clean on the trip. Lisa went into Prancer's stall with a set of shipping wraps and began to bandage Prancer's legs. Prancer stamped her feet impatiently and let out a high whinny.

"You know something's up, don't you, darling?"

18

Lisa said. She ran her hand down the mare's shoulder to soothe her. "It's a rally. I think you'll like it. Belle and Starlight will be there." Horses became accustomed to each other's company, and Lisa knew Prancer would be happy to be with her friends.

"Can we put Prancer in between Belle and Starlight?" Lisa called to Carole and Stevie. "I think that will help keep her relaxed."

"Sure," Stevie replied from Belle's stall, "if they let us decide which horse goes where."

Carole laughed. "I think they'll let us decide *everything*." She was rerolling one of her bandages to make it easier to put on Starlight's leg. As she walked past Danny's stall, she couldn't help looking inside. Carole was shocked. Danny wasn't wrapped and he wasn't wearing a sheet. From the flecks of hay across his withers, it didn't look as if he'd even been brushed that afternoon. And Veronica was standing in his stall, idly running a comb through his tangle-free mane.

"Better hurry," Carole told her. "Max will be here in fifteen minutes." If Veronica really got a move on, she might manage to have Danny ready in time.

Veronica gave her a stiff smile. "We're fine," she said.

Carole shrugged and walked on. Danny wasn't her job.

Bandaging a horse's legs took time, and Carole

19

was just finishing when she heard Max pull the big trailer into the yard. She pulled Starlight's leather show halter over his head and tied him to the post in his stall. "Be right back," she promised him.

In the aisle, Lisa was arranging their personal gear: three duffel bags, three sleeping bags, two pillows (Stevie never used one), three garment bags with their riding coats inside, and one very large plastic cooler. They would eat their meals with all the other competitors, but The Saddle Club had been to enough rallies to know they needed plenty of snacks.

Carole hefted one end of the cooler and helped Lisa carry it out to Max's truck. Max and Red began to load the heavier tack trunks. Meg, Betsy, and Stevie started loading gear, too. "Where's Veronica?" Max asked.

"Back with Danny," Meg told him.

Max seemed pleased until they started loading the horses. "Why aren't you ready?" he asked Veronica. Danny was still not brushed, blanketed, or wrapped.

"Sorry!" Meg said. "We didn't—" Max raised his hand to let Veronica speak.

Veronica looked apologetic. "I don't mean to hold everyone up," she said. "I just wasn't sure how to put Danny's shipping wraps on, and I knew I could hurt his legs if I did it wrong. I asked Carole, but she wouldn't help me."

"I beg your pardon!" Carole said. "You never—"

"Let's just get him ready," Max said firmly. Meg and Betsy hurried to help Veronica while Carole stood, astounded, outside the stall. Max gave Carole a quick squeeze on the shoulder and an encouraging look, and Carole felt much better. Max knew Veronica; he wouldn't believe her complaints.

When they got to the show grounds, they found that all the teams would be stabled in temporary stalls under a big tent. Each team was assigned four stalls: three for their horses and one as a combined tack room and living area for the riders. They would all camp out there overnight. Unfortunately, The Saddle Club girls found themselves in stalls right across an aisle from Veronica and her group.

"We'll make our tack room the outside stall," Veronica declared with a sniff. "That way we'll have at least some chance of fresh air. I can't believe they're making us sleep out in the stables. My mother was willing to put us up in a hotel, you know." She stood back as her family's chauffeur carried in a portable cot and air mattress.

"I can't stand it," Stevie muttered to Carole and Lisa. "My idea of fresh air is to be as far from Veronica as possible."

"I agree," said Lisa. They put Belle in the outside stall, then Prancer, then Starlight. Their tack room was on the inside of the row, right next to some stalls assigned to a team from another Pony Club.

21

"The water's at the end of the aisle, and somebody said extra shavings are at the other end of the tent," Carole reported. They all bustled about getting their horses' stalls ready. They hung water buckets and spread shavings. Carole broke open a bale of hay and split it among the three horses.

Max and Red had helped with the tack trunks again. Lisa saw them standing beside the truck, making jokes with one another. "Max, could you check to see if you think Prancer's got enough shavings?" she called to him. "The floor of her stall isn't very level. Does it matter?"

Max grinned at her and shook his head. "Can't help you," he said.

"Already?" Lisa asked. They'd just gotten there!

Max pointed to a pair of women walking through the tent with clipboards in their hands. Lisa gawked and rushed back to Stevie and Carole. "We're being inspected right now!" she said. "We're not set up!"

Carole calmly measured grain into Starlight's feed bucket. "Half the teams aren't set up. They must just be looking for things that people are doing wrong."

Lisa wasn't so sure. She anxiously finished Prancer's stall, then took Prancer's sheet off and hung it on their blanket rack in the tack room. Then she took it back down. What if Prancer needed it? The night was fairly warm, but it looked as if it might rain. Lisa wished she could ask Max for advice. She decided to ask Stevie. "Sheet or no sheet?"

Stevie looked up from inspecting Belle's hooves. "Sheet. It's going to storm."

From across the aisle they could hear Veronica's voice rising to a peevish whine. "What do you mean, I don't have my water bucket hung high enough? How high does a water bucket need to be?" Peeking out the doors of their horses' stalls, they saw the pair of inspectors talking to Veronica. They all ducked back, laughing.

"If she'd read her Pony Club manual, she'd know the answer to that question," Lisa said. "The water bucket has to be low enough that the horse can drink out of it but high enough that the horse can't knock it over or get a foot caught in it."

"And the bucket has to be tied to a post, not to a board in the stall," Stevie added. "The weight of a full bucket might pull a board loose, but it wouldn't hurt a post."

"What do you mean, I'm getting penalized?" Veronica shouted. Stevie and Lisa giggled.

"Poor sportsmanship," a voice chided them from the aisle. "Laughing at another team's errors."

They both looked out. "Phil!" Stevie cried. "I've been looking for you!"

Lisa saw A.J. and Bart standing behind Phil. "Hi, guys," she said brightly, stepping out into the aisle.

"Hi, Lisa," A.J. said. Bart just waved and smiled.

"We're two aisles down," Phil said, "on this same side. We've come to tell you to hurry. It's time for dinner, and rumor has it they're serving pizza."

"And we love pizza," A.J. said. "So we want to be sure to get first dibs. Right, Bart?"

"Right," Bart said. He gave Lisa another shy smile. Lisa felt herself starting to blush. How could she be so silly?

"I'll get Carole," Stevie said. "I think we're almost ready." She scurried down the aisle. Lisa looked at the three boys and struggled for something witty and clever to say.

"So, do you think it's going to rain?" she asked, just as a rumble of thunder sounded overhead. So much for witty and clever!

"Might," Bart said.

"Yeah," A.J. added, clapping Bart on the shoulder, "that's our friend Bart. King of the one-word answers."

Bart shrugged. He didn't look uncomfortable. "I do better with horses than people," he told Lisa.

"At least," Phil added teasingly, "he does better with horses than *girls*."

Bart blushed deep red, and Lisa felt herself blushing again, too. "Stevie!" she called out.

"Here we are!" Stevie said, coming out with Carole in tow. "Take us to your pizza!"

A crack of lightning lit the darkening sky, and rain began to pelt the roof of the tent. "Run!" Phil shouted. They took off across the field toward the mess hall, laughing. Lisa was immensely grateful not to have to look at Bart. She felt incredibly self-conscious. Did everyone notice her blush? And was that good or bad?

Lisa thought back to Bart's blush. Was he always that embarrassed around girls? Or was it possible that he was—at least a little—interested in her?

LISA SMACKED THE Off switch of her portable alarm clock to stop its ringing. She sat up in her sleeping bag and rubbed her eyes. Above her head, rain drummed steadily against the roof of the stabling tent, and the air smelled damp and cold. "Geez," she said, "did it rain all night?"

Carole stood up, shaking her sleeping bag loose, and leaned over the top of the tack room door. "Looks that way," she answered. "I can see a lot of puddles, including one right here in the middle of our aisle." They heard a thump from Starlight's stall, and Carole giggled. "Starlight sees me. He just butted his feed tub to tell me it's time for his break-fast."

They all got up, rolled their sleeping bags and stowed them neatly in a corner, and put on their socks and paddock boots. They had slept in sweat-shirts and old breeches. They divided the chores, Lisa getting the grain, Stevie the hay, and Carole the water.

"I'll be responsible for the water in more ways than one," Carole said. "I'm going to fill that aisle puddle before we go to breakfast. You never know when an inspector might come around." She grabbed a muck bucket and headed for the shavings pile.

Lisa toed the edge of the puddle. "Do you think the tent's leaking? I didn't feel a drop all night."

"Probably the rain just blew in from the side and settled in that low spot," Stevie guessed. "The whole aisle's muddy. We'll have to spread a lot of shav-ings."

Stevie dropped a flake of hay into each horse's stall. She paused to say good morning to Belle. "Hello, beautiful. Did you sleep well?" Belle looked fit and happy, but her hooves, Stevie noticed, were wet. Since Belle's stall was on the outside edge of the row, it had gotten pretty wet from rain blowing un-der the tent roof, and her bedding was soaked. Stevie knew that wet bedding wouldn't hurt a horse for a few hours, but it wasn't good for them as a regular thing. "I'm going to pick out this stall before breakfast," she said when Lisa came in with Belle's grain.

"Ugh," Lisa said, nodding agreement as her feet squished into the wet shavings. "Prancer's and Starlight's stalls are still dry."

"Good." Stevie pointed to Team Veronica's tack stall and grinned. "Do you think they got wet? I'd hate to have a little water disrupt Veronica's beauty sleep."

Lisa pursed her lips in thought. "I'm sure if Veronica had gotten wet, we would have heard all about it, even in the middle of the night. She's not the type to suffer in silence."

Stevie snorted. "You can say that again."

Lisa left. Stevie worked quickly, using a pitchfork to scoop the wet bedding into one of their muck buckets. Then she dragged the muck bucket through the diminishing rain to the place where they were supposed to pile used bedding. It took three trips before Belle's stall was stripped. Then Stevie took the big bucket to the shavings pile and started filling it. When she returned to Belle's stall, an inspector was looking over the door, pencil and clipboard in hand.

When she saw Stevie she shook her head. "I'm going to have to give you some penalty points for that," she said.

28

Stevie's jaw dropped. "But it rained all night, and I'm fixing it right now! I'm working as quickly as I can!"

The woman shook her head and pointed to Belle's tail with her pencil. "I mean that, not the stall."

Stevie looked. Belle's tail, which only the night before had been a black, shining, tangle-free flow of hair, now hung in a stiff, dirty, matted clump. "Belle!" Stevie said in astonishment. She put her hand on Belle's hip and gently picked up her tail. What had Belle done? Turned out to pasture, horses sometimes got burrs or weeds matted into their tails, but Belle had been safe inside all night. Stevie's fingers pried the clump apart. The middle was mud— pure, filthy, dried mud. And Belle's floor, although damp, had been covered with shavings. There wasn't any mud in sight.

Stevie looked over the door of Belle's stall. Veronica was coming out of her tack room, makeup kit in hand. She hurried down the aisle without meeting Stevie's eyes.

Veronica! I might have known! Stevie's first thought was to see how Veronica liked getting mud in *her* hair. Her second thought was to tell the show officials, but she knew she had no proof. A mud ball was the sort of thing that could happen if Belle was turned out and not groomed regularly. The fact that

Stevie would never allow it to happen was something else Stevie knew she couldn't prove.

Stevie called Lisa and Carole into the stall. "Look what just cost us some points," she said grimly.

"Stevie!" Lisa was appalled. "How could that happen?"

"I think I know." Stevie gestured to the stalls across the aisle.

"Meg and Betsy would never—" Carole began.

"No," Stevie said. "They wouldn't."

Lisa and Carole didn't say anything. They all knew that Veronica would stoop to dirty tricks—even to cheating—to show up The Saddle Club.

"With a horse like Danny, she still thinks she has to do something like this! Poor Belle!" Carole stroked the mare's nose. "We can't prove it, though, can we? I never saw Veronica—or anyone else—go into Belle's stall."

"Me either," Lisa said. "I guess it's sort of a compliment: She thinks we're going to be so hard to beat that she has to sabotage our chances."

"Yeah, right," Stevie snorted. She fetched a comb from her grooming box and started to work the mud out of Belle's tail. "I feel complimented, all right. And I'll tell you what, I'm not leaving for breakfast until Veronica does. I'm not giving her another chance."

"We'll all keep an eye on her," Carole promised.

"For now, Lisa and I will finish up out here. When you're done with Belle we'll go to breakfast."

Carole made sure that the other stalls were in good order. Lisa offered to straighten the tack room. When Stevie finished, she and Carole went into the tack room, where they discovered that Lisa had changed into a clean sweatshirt. She'd brushed her hair into a neat ponytail and tied a ribbon around it, and she was using a small hand mirror to apply lip gloss.

"Whoa!" Carole said. "Lisa, they're not inspecting us until right before we ride."

"Yeah," added Stevie, "and I don't think they give extra credit for lip gloss."

Lisa half hid the mirror behind her back. She blushed and looked at the ground. "I just didn't feel like looking so grubby," she said.

"Who would notice?" Stevie said, indicating her own dirt-stained sweatshirt. Then she understood. "Ah," she said. "That's the question, isn't it? Who might notice? More to the point, who were you *hoping* would notice?"

Lisa blushed deeper red. She turned and stowed her lip gloss and mirror into her duffel bag, then firmly zipped the bag. Carole took another step inside the tack stall and pulled the curtain across the doorway. "Lisa," she said gently, "you can tell us anything."

31

Lisa grinned. "I know, it's just a little embarrassing. But lately I've noticed—I mean, don't you think Phil's friend Bart is kind of cute?"

Carole had never really thought about Bart one way or another, but she was instantly supportive. "He seems like a nice guy. He's quiet, but he's great around horses."

Lisa nodded. She knew that was about the highest compliment Carole could give another person.

"So . . . ," Stevie said.

"So I was thinking about asking him to the dance," Lisa confessed in a rush. "I don't know him that well, but I'd like to know him better, and that would be a good chance. And it would be fun. And—I'd like to, that's all. But I've hardly got the nerve to say that to you guys. I don't know how I'll ever actually say anything to Bart. I was hoping that looking nice would help me feel more confident."

"It couldn't hurt," Carole said. "Look, why don't the three of us make a point of inviting the three of them? That way it won't be so embarrassing, and you'll still get to spend time with him at the dance and get to know him better."

"Phil's already coming," Stevie protested. "He knows all about it."

"Well, of course," Carole retorted. "That makes it even easier. Phil's coming, so A.J. and Bart will want to, too."

"That would be super," Lisa said. "Thank you. I don't know why this sort of thing is so hard."

"We'll make it easier," Stevie said. "The Saddle Club always sticks together."

"You bet," said Carole.

LISA SIGHED. "GUESS I got all dressed up for nothing."
Her friends laughed. Even though Lisa looked better
than they did, she hardly looked "all dressed up."

"I wouldn't say for nothing," Stevie teased. "Carole and I certainly appreciated your efforts."

Lisa grinned. "Good. At least I know *you'll* go to
the dance with me."

"But of course," said Stevie.

Lisa knew she shouldn't feel so tense. What was
one little dance, after all? But she was disappointed
that she hadn't seen Bart, or Phil, or A.J. at breakfast. Breakfast was served buffet style, whenever the

Pony Clubbers were ready for it. The boys must have eaten early; they weren't anywhere in sight.

"I'll bet Mr. Baker had them do their course walk early," Stevie guessed. "Phil said he was going to be one of the first on the course this morning." At real combined training competitions, dressage usually went before cross-country, but at this rally, they were all doing cross-country first. Dressage would be held in late afternoon, and show jumping on Sunday morning. In addition, all the competitors had to take a written test on horse care after the show jumping.

Lisa scuffed her feet through the wet grass. "I wish I were riding earlier. All this rain is going to make the ground in front of the fences muddy, and it's just going to get worse throughout the day."

"Unless the sun comes out," Carole said. "The rain's stopped, anyway. That's something."

Lisa shook her head, and Carole looked at her sympathetically. Mud bothered Prancer; she didn't like to get her feet dirty.

"Maybe Max will have some suggestions," Carole said. The riders had a few hours to walk the course on foot with their instructors, who could give them suggestions on how to ride it with their horses. The course walk was the only time all weekend that they were allowed adult assistance. Carole vowed to learn as much as possible during it. Starlight would be counting on her.

"Too bad we have to share Max with Team Veronica," Stevie muttered. "She'll probably spend her time making mud balls. It's not as if she'll be listening to Max."

The Saddle Club ducked into the stabling tent to check on their horses, then joined Max, who was standing just outside with Team Veronica.

"No new sabotage," Stevie reported to Lisa in an undertone. "But Belle's tail still looks awful. It's going to take me days to get it really clean."

Veronica had a map in her hand and was showing it to Max. "See?" she said in a sweet voice. "This is our official course. It says exactly which jumps we should take. There are a lot of jumps on this property, so we'll have to be careful."

Max folded the map and put it in his pocket. "Thank you. That'll be helpful." He rubbed his hands and looked at the six riders. "Ready to go?" They started walking across the wet field.

"Like we need a map," Stevie whispered. "The fences are numbered, and the ones for our course have green flags." She gave Veronica a venomous look and said more loudly, "My, Veronica, your hair looks lovely today. However do you keep it so clean?"

Veronica flipped her hair back and gave Stevie a

36

wide smile. "Regular salon treatment does help, of course. But *you* might see a difference if you simply used shampoo."

Stevie started to say more, but Carole gave her a swift poke. They had reached the first fence, a simple log jump. The first fences on cross-country courses were usually straightforward to encourage the horses to go on. Max didn't have much to say about this fence, except to remind them all to establish an even pace early. Lisa stomped around the approach to the jump. The ground there was already very soft. The hooves from the first few horses would churn it into mud.

"Oh no," Stevie groaned. The second jump was less than a hundred yards after the first—and it was a coop. Stevie had expected coop jumps, but she had hoped not to have any until at least the middle of the course, when Belle would be fully warmed up.

Carole frowned. The approach to the coop was tricky; the course curved in front of it to avoid some large trees, and woods started just after the fence, so that the horses would feel as if they were jumping into the woods. She would have to ride a careful line and give Starlight plenty of encouragement.

"It's going to be very important that we not over-shoot the turn, isn't it, Max?" Veronica asked. "I mean, if we don't straighten the horses out after we go around the trees, they might keep turning and run past the side of the fence, the way Barq tried to with Meg during our last lesson."

Max smiled. "That's exactly right. All of you should find something to aim at—a tree or fence post—so that you know you've got your horse steered correctly. Run-outs will be common here."

"Just what I need," Stevie said. "A coop that encourages the horse not to jump." She climbed on top of the sturdy fence. "It's a chicken coop!" she said. "It turns the horses into chickens!"

"Stevie, get down from there," Max said sternly. "Quit fooling around."

"Just seeing if the jump looks any better from up here," Stevie said. "It doesn't."

"It's not a very high jump," Veronica said, measuring it against her leg. "I can't imagine any horse having trouble clearing it."

"Right," Max said. "It's only two feet, six inches. Our coop at home is higher."

Max gave Veronica another approving smile. Carole guessed that he was glad to see Veronica act like a person who actually knew about, and cared about, the course she would be riding. Carole could think of two reasons for Veronica's sudden good-rider attitude. One, Veronica's first horse, a beautiful Thoroughbred name Cobalt, had died after a cross-country accident caused by Veronica's jumping him carelessly. Cobalt's death had been the one thing that had really seemed to sink into Veronica's salon-groomed head; afterward, she always tried her best to ride well cross-country.

But two, Carole thought, Veronica was sucking up. Danny was so good that Veronica could ride the course blindfolded and they would do well. She didn't have to worry about setting Danny up for the jumps. He was almost guaranteed to do well. Veronica just wanted to look good compared to The Saddle Club.

And she did. Carole was so preoccupied with the landing side of the coop that she walked right into Max. "Sorry," she said.

"That's all right," Max said. "The trail forks here, as you see. Which side do we take?"

Carole looked at the trails in confusion. *Shouldn't there be a sign?* "I don't know," she said.

"Well"—Max pulled Veronica's map out of his pocket with a flourish—"this is where a little preparation comes in handy."

Carole blushed. She was preparing right now—she was walking the course. And she would have figured out which trail to take long before she had started out with Starlight.

"It's the left-hand fork," Meg piped up. "Veronica showed me."

"What else has she showed you today?" Stevie asked. "Any handy ways of causing opposing teams to be penalized?"

Meg frowned. "What are you talking about?"

Lisa understood—mud. The approach to the coop had absorbed her attention, but as soon as she thought the word *mud*, she was back to worrying about the footing. She didn't notice the quelling look Max gave Stevie.

They continued on the course. Stevie felt so worried she was almost petrified. Even jumps that weren't actually coops were starting to look like coops to her. The fourth jump was a bank—basically, a small hill that the horses jumped onto instead of over. *What is a bank*, Stevie thought wildly, *but half a coop covered with grass?* "Veronica, you won't have any trouble here," she called out gaily to mask her rising anxiety. "You know all about *banks*." Stevie thought that was pretty funny, given that Veronica's dad was a banker, but no one else laughed. Even Carole looked at her strangely.

Veronica started to climb to the top of the bank. "Hey, Max!" Stevie cried. "Now *Veronica's* climbing on the jumps!"

Veronica shot her a cold look. "I'm just checking to see how the footing is up here," she explained to Max. "After all, the horses land on top of this. Betsy, don't you think you'd better check? Coconut's so funny about soft footing."

"Good thinking, Veronica," Max praised her. "And it's smart of you to consider your teammates' horses as well as your own."

Carole shook her head ruefully. Veronica had made a good point. Why hadn't *she* thought of it? Carole remembered reading about a competition that had installed a new bank and hadn't given the top of it time to settle. The first horse on course had sunk up to its elbows.

Lisa, suddenly concerned with how Prancer would handle the footing, climbed up on the bank, too. Meg offered her a hand. To Lisa's relief, the top of the bank was solid and well-drained, nearly dry. Stevie made some other rude comment to Veronica, and in the back of her mind Lisa thought Stevie was starting to get out of hand. The front of her mind, however, was still occupied with the course. She didn't say anything to her friend.

At the water complex, a gently flowing stream with a few low jumps on either side, Stevie asked Veronica if she didn't feel like taking a swim. "Might wash the mud off your hands," she said.

Veronica looked up, and for a moment Carole thought she saw total comprehension in Veronica's eyes. But the other girl just answered innocently, "I

THE SADDLE CLUB

don't know what you're talking about, Stevie Lake, but you're starting to get on my nerves."

"And mine!" boomed Max. "Really, Stevie, if you'd spend half as much time studying the course as you do making jokes, you wouldn't have anything to worry about. Veronica's planned for this competition, and she's been a help to everyone. Furthermore, her conduct, unlike yours, has shown real Pony Club spirit."

Stevie, her face burning red, was silent. She was embarrassed to have Max yell at her, but beyond that, she was so furious she couldn't speak for a moment. Max nodded at her, then began walking toward the next jump. "It's spirit, all right," she whispered. "Creating all the trouble you can for other teams, that's real spirit—real *Veronica* spirit."

"What are you *talking* about?" Meg asked again.

"Don't pay her any attention," Veronica said, lifting her nose into the air. "It wasn't my fault Belle got mud in her tail," she said to Stevie. "Maybe you ought to spend a little less time assigning blame to other people and a little more time taking care of your poor horse."

"*My poor horse!* What about you, who always lets everyone else take care of Danny?" Stevie was so upset she leaned right into Veronica's face. Veronica stepped backward to the edge of the stream.

"Really!" Carole added, rushing to Stevie's de-

42

fense. "You didn't even know how to wrap Danny's legs—or else you were too lazy to do it."

"I ought to push you right into the stream! How'd you like a bath?" Stevie said.

"Stevie!" Max roared. "Carole! Veronica! All of you girls, *I am ashamed!*"

Stevie dropped her arms to her sides. Carole went still. Only Veronica continued to speak. "I don't know what they're talking about," she told Max.

"Unfortunately," Max said, "I do. But that's irrelevant to the current situation. Hear this, all of you: Any rider who says anything—I mean *anything*—during the rest of this walk not directly connected to this course and how it should be ridden will be expelled from this event and suspended from Horse Wise. Don't test me to see if I mean it. I don't want to hear a single word until we get back to the stabling area and you six are on your own again. Understood?"

"Yes, Max," they all mumbled. Lisa had never seen him so furious. Max didn't often lose his temper, but when he did, it took him a while to find it again. They were all very quiet for the rest of the course walk. Even when the last jump turned out to be another coop, Stevie only patted it sadly and said nothing.

Back at the stalls, Carole grabbed Stevie's arm and

hustled her into their tack room before she could get another shot at Veronica. "Not a word," she said. "Not to Veronica, Meg, or Betsy, for the rest of the weekend, from any of us. I was never so embarrassed, Stevie. Max shouldn't have had to talk to us like that."

Stevie hung her head. She sat down on her tack trunk and looked up at Carole. "I know," she said. "But this is going to be an awful day. There are too many coops out there. Belle's going to be eliminated, and then we won't even get a team score."

"She'll be fine," Lisa said, sitting down next to Stevie. "Remember how much she loves you. She'll jump anything if she thinks she's jumping it for you."

"I just don't have the guts," Stevie said. "I look at those jumps and I think, *Wow, that's big,* and as soon as I've thought *that,* I'm as good as finished. Plus, I'm really angry that someone would do that to Belle. It couldn't have been comfortable for her to have mud drying in her tail all night."

"I know," Lisa said soothingly.

"We don't have proof that Veronica did it," Carole reminded them.

Stevie's eyes grew wide with sudden realization. "Yes we do! Remember what she said—that it wasn't her fault Belle got mud in her tail? I didn't tell anyone what happened except for the two of you! How would she know if she hadn't done it herself?"

Lisa shook her head. "She might have looked into the stall in the morning and seen it," she said.

"She woke up after us," Stevie said. "Remember?"

"At least," Carole said, "she gave the impression that she woke up after us. But I agree with you, Stevie. I think Veronica probably did it."

"I'm going to kill her," Stevie said.

"Not until after the competition is over," Carole said. "Max means it—he'll kick us out. Promise me, Stevie."

Stevie looked at her friend's solemn face. "Oh, I promise," she said. "Don't worry, Carole. I won't get us eliminated for any other reason than Belle's refusal to jump coops. Beating Veronica would still be the best revenge. But when we get back to Pine Hollow, look out!"

They had only an hour to get ready for their horse inspection and cross-country ride. They began by giving their horses a thorough grooming. Lisa had just stepped out of Prancer's stall when she saw Phil, A.J., and Bart walk past with water buckets in their hands. Lisa latched Prancer's door and went after them.

"Hey!" she said. "Wait up!" When they stopped

and turned around, she smiled at them. Bart had the cutest eyes and a really nice nose, she decided. As soon as she thought that, she felt butterflies begin to hatch in her stomach.

"Hey," she said again. She took a deep breath. This was so hard! She made herself look at Phil, since he seemed safest. "Our school's having this great dance next Friday," she said. "It's going to be held outside, so we can invite anyone we want. Would you all like to come?" She gave Bart a quick smile. Carole was right, she thought gratefully, it was much easier to invite all of them than Bart alone.

"I'll be there," Phil said with a quick wink. Lisa grinned at him. She already knew he was coming.

"Hey, me too," said A.J. "Sounds fun. What about you?" He gave Bart a poke.

Bart turned slightly pink and looked over at the stalls next to Lisa. "Um, maybe," he said at last. "I might have to go visit my cousin that night. I'm not sure."

Lisa tried to keep the smile firmly on her face until they were gone. It was all she could do not to show how hurt and embarrassed she was. Might have to visit his cousin! What a lame excuse! Bart might just as well have said he wasn't interested in the dance or Lisa, either.

Carole came up to Lisa's shoulder. "What's wrong?" she asked.

Lisa blew a deep breath. "This day just has to get better," she said. "It can't get a whole lot worse."

"Good luck, Betsy!" Lisa called. Across the aisle Betsy, completely outfitted for her cross-country ride, led a gleaming Coconut out of the stall. Even though Lisa devoutly hoped that The Saddle Club would beat Betsy and Team Veronica, she really did wish Betsy well. Cross-country courses were nerve-racking. Lisa herself was dressed for her ride; she had just started to saddle Prancer.

"Thanks," Betsy said a little nervously. "I wish we had a good-luck horseshoe here like we do at Pine Hollow." She smiled at Lisa, and Lisa smiled back. She watched Betsy lead Coconut down the grassy slope beside the stables to where the formal inspections were taking place. Before being allowed to start cross-country, each rider and horse and their gear were thoroughly evaluated for safety, suitability, and cleanliness. Betsy looked great, and so had Meg, who was already riding the course.

Lisa wasn't very worried about her inspection. It was something every careful rider should be able to pass with ease. At the same time, since all the competitors ought to be able to do well, if they got any penalties during inspection, they had reason to feel ashamed. Lisa vowed not to disgrace herself or Prancer. She settled her saddle over Prancer's back, being especially careful to smooth out any folds in the pads.

"Lisa? How do we look?" Carole brought Starlight out into the aisle. She would ride first for The Saddle Club. Veronica would ride right after Carole, then Lisa two riders later, then Stevie.

"Fantastic!" Lisa said with true admiration. Starlight's coat gleamed with the shine that could only come from regular grooming. His tack was in perfect condition. Carole looked as neat as her horse. "Only . . ." Lisa flicked a spot of mud from Carole's boot.

"Thanks," Carole said. "Can you look us over again once we get outside?"

"Of course," Lisa said. She followed Starlight into the sunlight, then took a towel from Carole and carefully smoothed the dust from the horse's flanks. "Professional," she said to her friend.

"Carole Hanson and Starlight," came a voice over the PA system. Lisa gave Carole a quick hug. She would have liked to stay and watch her friend get started on the course, but she knew her turn was coming up fast. She'd be in trouble if she wasn't ready in time.

In the stables, Stevie had been about to follow Lisa and Carole outside when a horrendous shrieking stopped her in her tracks. "Help me, help me, *help me!*" the voice cried, each word louder and more anguished than before. It was coming from Team Veronica's tack room, where Veronica was dressing alone, and from the pitch and volume of the shrieks it sounded as if Veronica was being killed.

Maybe a giant poisonous spider has bitten her right on the nose, Stevie thought with radiant hope. *Or maybe a rat.* Yes, Stevie *definitely* hoped it was a rat—a big, brown, ugly, obese, vicious one curled up in one of the toes of Veronica's custom-made boots. It would serve her right.

"Help me!" Veronica cried again. Stevie sighed, dropped her grooming mitt into a bucket, and ducked under the curtain tacked across the doorway of the stall. Max would expect her to help. He would insist on it. Besides, if there really was a rat in Veronica's boot, Stevie didn't want to miss it.

"What's wrong?" she asked. Veronica was hopping up and down in the center of the room, tugging at something on the back of her neck. She was already wearing her boots, so it couldn't be a rat. Stevie hoped for the spider instead.

"My hair's caught!" Veronica moaned. "Oh, I'm in pain!" When Stevie tried to look, Veronica swatted her hand away. "You're hurting me!"

"Quit jumping around!" Stevie said. "Here. Hold still." The back of Veronica's hair net and a few strands of her silky black hair had gotten tangled in the Velcro fastener at the back of her shirt collar. Stevie pulled it free.

"Ouch!" Veronica said. "You yanked my hair out."

"Better than leaving you stuck," Stevie retorted. She could hardly believe that even Veronica would make such a big fuss over such a little problem.

Veronica sniffed. "I just can't believe Meg and Betsy would leave me here to get ready all by myself."

"They're riding," Stevie said impatiently. What did Veronica expect? It occurred to Stevie that she hadn't seen Veronica help either Meg or Betsy get ready.

"I asked Meg to polish my boots for me last night and she wouldn't even do that," Veronica complained. "I thought they were my friends. Danny and I are going to carry them through this entire competition, but they act like I'm still supposed to be *working* around here."

"Too bad," Stevie said, her voice dripping with sarcasm. "Think what a little work would do to your reputation." She turned on her heel, then saw something that made her pause. "Veronica," she said seriously, "have you noticed your bridle rack?"

"Of course," Veronica said. "Daddy bought it for me in Italy. It's handmade."

"It's falling," Stevie said. "You've got it tied up here with a piece of old baling twine, and the twine's about to break. And look—there's a great big mud puddle underneath it." The rack was hung on the outer wall of the stall, right above a low spot where rain had come in overnight. Danny's bridle, breastplate, and martingale all hung from it.

"You need to put some shavings in that puddle," Stevie told Veronica. "Then, if you can find some wire or some stronger rope, I'll help you fix the rack."

Veronica flicked an impatient hand at Stevie. "Go fix it yourself if you want everything perfect," she said. "You're as picky as Betsy and Meg. Now go away. I need to get ready."

Stevie shut her lips very firmly and counted to ten as she walked out of the stall. She had promised Max she would behave. She had promised Carole she wouldn't murder Veronica until they were back at Pine Hollow.

"What's wrong?" Lisa asked, coming back to the tent.

"Just remind me when we get back home that there's something I need to do," Stevie said. "Where's Carole? I hope she hasn't left yet."

"No—she's in the inspection. I wanted to stay, but I'm only a few riders away. I just heard one of the inspectors ask Carole why Starlight is wearing a double-jointed bit and how she knows that it fits him correctly."

Stevie grinned. "For Carole, those are easy questions."

"Yeah," Lisa said, "but not for me. This looks a little harder than I thought."

"I want to say good-bye to Carole," Stevie said. "Do you need any help right now?"

"No, go," Lisa said. "Just wish me luck first. I'm two riders after Veronica, and she's right after Carole."

"I'll stay and watch you start off, too," Stevie promised. "Belle is practically ready, and there are five riders between me and you."

"Hey," Lisa said, remembering, "who was that calling for help a few minutes ago? Sounded like someone put a nail through her foot."

53

Stevie shook her head. "It was just a rat."

Outside, Carole saw Stevie approach out of the corner of her eye. She turned her head a little so that she could wink at her friend. Even though the inspectors were being a little more thorough than Carole had anticipated, they weren't making her nervous. She knew everything there was to know about Starlight's care, and she was proud of how beautiful and well-groomed he looked. Even the competition wasn't scaring her now that she was this close to it. Win or lose, it would be another learning experience for her and Starlight.

Carole thought she heard a muffled scream coming from the stabling tent. She hoped it wasn't Lisa.

"All right," one of the inspectors said. "You're clear." She smiled at Carole. Another scream, louder this time, came from the stabling tent. Both inspectors paused and looked up the hill with concern. "Um, well," the first said again to Carole, "you're finished, but you'll have to wait a few minutes before you can ride. The starter's backed up. Mount and be ready, and he'll call your name."

"Thank you," Carole said, at the same time as someone yelled, "My saddle! *Ayyyyhi!*" The last word sounded like a wolf howling.

"Well," the first inspector said to the second, "if it's a saddle problem, it probably isn't a broken bone or a concussion. Who's the next rider?" She picked up a microphone.

Carole moved Starlight to the side. Stevie gave her a leg up just as one of the inspectors called, "Veronica diAngelo," over the loudspeaker. No one came out of the now silent stable tent. A full minute passed.

"Veronica diAngelo, please report to inspection," the inspector called again, more firmly. "This is your second call."

"Wow," Carole whispered to Stevie. "Where do you think she is? Three calls and you're out. She'll be eliminated if she doesn't get out here."

"She was getting dressed," Stevie whispered back. "Danny wasn't tacked, but he was clean." She looked back at the stable and then up at Carole and Starlight. "Don't get distracted. Think about the course."

Carole nodded toward the starting box. "I think I've got a little while to wait. Someone out there must be having a problem." Usually the starters sent a new rider out every five minutes, but now two other riders, and Carole, were waiting their turns. If one of the riders on course had fallen off, or if a horse had gotten loose, the officials wouldn't allow anyone else to start until the problem had been fixed.

The inspector was on the point of announcing Veronica's name for the third and final time when a rider walked out of the tent. The inspector smiled and put down her microphone. "That's not Veronica," Stevie said. "That's Lisa!"

Lisa's face was pale and her eyes held an expression of horror mixed with the faintest touch of amusement. "Veronica will be right out," she said politely. "She's coming—she's just had a little disaster."

When Veronica appeared with Danny, it became clear that the word *little* in no way described the disaster that had befallen her. The near side of Veronica's gorgeous saddle looked at first as though it had been dipped in chocolate—and then Carole realized that the chocolate was actually *mud*. Mud coated Danny's bridle and breastplate, too, and was in the process of getting all over his once spotless gray coat. As Carole watched, horrified, a big splotch of gooey mud slid off one of Danny's stirrup leathers and caught Veronica right on the thigh. It was obvious to Carole that Veronica had tried to wipe her tack off, but the mud was too pervasive. Cleanup would take hours.

Veronica herself looked just as wrecked. Her clothes were so filthy it looked as if she'd worn them for weeks. Her hair was coming out of its net, and her helmet was askew. She was wearing only one glove. "Why won't anyone help me?" she screamed.

"I tried to help her," Lisa whispered indignantly to Carole and Stevie. "She actually threatened me with her crop. She told me this was my fault—and I was in Prancer's stall the whole time!"

"What happened?" Carole asked.

"I think when she took her saddle out of her trunk she tried to hang it on her bridle rack," Lisa reported. "The rack collapsed, and the tack went everywhere—"

"Right into that big mud puddle," Stevie finished. "I saw it," she added in response to her friends' questioning looks. "I even told Veronica she ought to fix it, and the bridle rack, too. It was an accident in progress, all right. But no, I didn't cause any of it. I told you I'd wait until we got home."

Carole and Lisa nodded, satisfied, then turned their attention back to the inspection area. The scene that was unfolding before them was awe-inspiring. Veronica had been so upset by the accident that she had gotten her girth twisted and put her breastplate on backward. When the inspectors pointed these major faults out to her, she flew into a rage.

"What do you mean, you're going to have to penalize me?" she shouted in her haughtiest, most di-

Angelo voice. "You can't penalize a person because of a little mud!"

"Riding with a twisted girth is a hazard to both the rider and the horse," the second inspector said clearly. "Your saddle would have come loose while you were galloping, and the twist would have given your horse a gall."

"So?" Veronica said. "I'll fix it before I ride—you can't penalize me for something I've fixed!" She grabbed the checklist out of the first inspector's hands and read what was written there. "You can't penalize me for *dirt!*" she continued, her voice rising to decibel levels it had never reached in her thirteen years of throwing tantrums. "I wasn't dirty five min-utes ago! My groom cleaned this tack three times last week! This isn't my fault! How dare you give me penalties! Don't you know who I am?"

"They do now," Lisa whispered to her friends. "And I'm sure they'll never forget."

"She's going for the All-Time Horse Inspection Penalty Record," Stevie whispered. "I bet she couldn't get any more points if she threw up on the inspectors."

Carole laughed despite herself. She put her hand over her mouth and tried to turn the laugh into a cough, but Veronica heard.

"You!" she said, pointing a dirty, ungloved finger up at Carole. "You and your two friends! You must have planned this. That's who did it," she said to the inspectors. "The Saddle Club—they're behind everything. It's their fault, not mine!"

One of the inspectors put out a hand to restrain Veronica. Carole rode Starlight a little way away, and Lisa and Stevie followed her. "I'm sorry she thinks that," Carole said. "I might want to do something like that to Veronica, but I would never do that to Danny. Think how uncomfortable he must be."

"And even I've never come up with such an effective plan for revenge," Stevie said. She looked over at Veronica and the two inspectors, who were now fully engaged in an argument. The head of the rally was running toward them, and Stevie thought she saw Max detach himself from the gathering crowd. "This is Super Revenge," Stevie said. "I hate to admit it, but this would have been beyond me. Danny has finally met his match. He's been beaten by Veronica herself."

6

CAROLE RODE WITH her seat just out of the saddle, her weight sinking evenly into her heels. She kept her hands steady against Starlight's neck. He was galloping smoothly, confidently, with his head high and his eyes alert, watching for the next jump but not fearing it. Carole felt her heart leap. They were halfway through the cross-country course and Starlight had yet to put a foot wrong. Better still, his attitude was telling her that he was enjoying this ride as much as she was. They were on the same wavelength; they understood the same things. To Carole, there was no greater joy. All the blue ribbons in the world couldn't beat feeling one with your horse.

The course curved. Carole turned Starlight by shifting her weight slightly in the saddle. She gathered her reins and steadied him for the approaching jump. It was a coop, the kind of jump Stevie was so afraid of. Carole bit her lip as Starlight sailed over it. She hoped Stevie would do okay. Then she thought of Stevie as she last saw her, standing near a hysterical, filthy Veronica. She bit her lip harder. It wasn't very nice to laugh at Veronica's predicament—but it was hard not to.

They galloped around a corner and Starlight tossed his head. The next jump came up much more quickly than Carole remembered and she didn't really have enough time to prepare her horse. She grabbed Starlight's mane with both hands and urged him forward with her legs. He jumped the fence awkwardly, but he made it over, which was all the judges cared about. "Sorry, buddy," Carole said, reaching down to pat his neck before resuming her galloping position. She had to keep her mind on the course.

AT THE STARTING BOX, Stevie waited her turn. She'd passed the inspection easily, checked her girth, and mounted. Now she walked Belle in circles to keep the horse calm. Stevie felt remarkably calm. In fact, she couldn't remember feeling this calm before a competition.

Betsy galloped across the finish line, which was next to the starting box. She pulled Coconut up and patted the horse's neck briskly.

"Hey," Stevie called to her.

"How'd it go?" another voice behind Stevie asked. Stevie turned to see Meg walking a sweating Barq in the grassy field behind the inspection area. Stevie hadn't noticed them before.

Betsy rode over to Meg and dismounted, and Meg helped her loosen the girth and run up the stirrups. Stevie checked her position. She still had a few riders to go, so she walked Belle over to Barq and Coconut.

"It went pretty well," Betsy said. She wiped the sweat from her face. "Coconut got a little more excited than I expected. Maybe I should have used a pelham bit, I don't know. We had a refusal once because I just couldn't slow us down enough to point Coconut at the jump—we went right around it." She laughed. "We sure didn't get any time penalties, though."

Meg nodded. "We had one refusal, too. That jump going into the woods. I don't think Barq could see it properly—he just put the brakes on. But I've heard that most people are having trouble out there."

"Have you heard about Veronica?" Stevie asked.

"What about Veronica?" said Meg, frowning.

"She's on course, isn't she? She was gone when I came in."

"Yeah, she's out there." Stevie couldn't quite keep a note of satisfaction out of her voice, even though, for Meg's and Betsy's sakes, she didn't want to rub it in. Briefly she filled them in on Veronica's disaster.

Meg looked more agitated than horrified. "I told her three times to fill in that mud puddle," she said. "I didn't have time to do it—I spent my whole morning doing her work as well as my own."

"We should have checked that bridle rack," Betsy said. "Hanging it was one of the few things Veronica did on her own."

"But who would think she couldn't hang a bridle rack?" snorted Meg. "It's not exactly rocket science."

"Sometimes she's just not worth it," Betsy added. "She pulls that princess act just a little too often. Sometimes I feel like we're Cinderella or something, put on this earth to do her work while she goes off to the ball."

"Cinderella ends up being the princess," Stevie said. "Remember?"

"Whatever," Meg said. "It doesn't matter—it doesn't change Veronica. You watch. When she comes in, she'll expect Betsy and me to clean all her filthy tack. She'll sit on her cot and moan about how the mud ruined her hair."

"There's Carole," Betsy said. "She looks happy."

Carole galloped in with a radiant glow on her face that Stevie had seen often. Stevie rode over to her friend's side. "Another good round?" she asked.

"He was so fantastic!" Carole dismounted and hugged Starlight. "Aren't you going yet, Stevie?"

"There's been another hold on course," Stevie reported.

Carole frowned. "I hope it wasn't Lisa."

"Nope," said Stevie, looking toward the woods. "Here she comes."

When Lisa galloped over the finish line, her friends knew how well she'd done before she even pulled up. Her face was glowing. "We've never done that well," Lisa gasped. "Never. She listened to me the entire time." Stevie and Carole cheered, and they exchanged high fives.

"Three cheers for The Saddle Club!" Stevie said, laughing. "Hope I can uphold our honor."

Lisa dismounted, and she and Carole began to care for their horses. "Are you still nervous?" Lisa asked sympathetically.

"No," Stevie said. "I know it sounds bizarre, but all my worries just seemed to go away the moment I saw dear Veronica with mud all over her Hermès saddle and custom-made boots. Apparently that was just the tonic I needed."

To Lisa this made some sense. She remembered

the lesson they'd had Tuesday, when Belle had refused to jump. Veronica's constant needling had been one of the things that set Stevie's nerves on edge.

Belle fretted and danced. Stevie eyed the starter impatiently. Finally, after a long delay, he started sending riders off again. Stevie was almost ready to ride.

Lisa and Carole walked their horses as close to the starting box as possible so that they could see Stevie go. Carole was examining a tiny cut on Starlight's knee when she heard Stevie say, in a voice of awe, "That hold on course—it must have been for *Veronica*." Veronica was trotting Danny out of the woods. Danny had his ears back and looked miserable, and Veronica was kicking him in fury.

"Of course," Lisa said instantly. "She started in front of me—I shouldn't have been able to pass her. I hadn't even thought. What happened?"

"Do you suppose she fell off?"

"Why wouldn't I have seen her?" Lisa asked. "Why wouldn't the jump judges have stopped me?" Lisa hoped she hadn't done anything wrong.

"She looks awful," Carole said. "I've never seen her so angry."

"Stevie Lake!" announced the starter.

"Gotta go!" Stevie said cheerfully. She waved her crop at her friends, then, on the starter's count, gal-

65

loped Belle off. Lisa and Carole continued to look in amazement at Veronica. Danny wasn't limping—he didn't seem to be hurt in any way—but he did seem for once to be absolutely fed up with his rider. As soon as he had crossed the finish line, he stopped and refused to carry her any farther. Veronica screamed in rage. She went to hit him with her crop, but the crop flew out of her hand and narrowly missed hitting an official.

"She must have gone off course," Lisa said. "She must have turned the wrong way and jumped the wrong jumps. Otherwise I couldn't have gotten around her."

Carole nodded. Veronica had dismounted and was screaming at the official, who had confiscated her crop. "I think it's time we took these horses back to their stalls," she said to Lisa. "I don't think we need to see Veronica for the next few minutes."

Lisa nodded. "Plus, I know a few horses who deserve baths and a pound of carrots apiece."

Carole grinned. "Agreed."

CAROLE AND LISA had their horses bathed and were drying them in front of the stabling tent when Stevie finished the course. She rode Belle right up to them. "Hey," she called, "want to hear some good news? Sixteen of the twenty teams have completed cross-country. One—just one—has a perfect score. Guess

66

which team that is?" Stevie's broad grin told them the answer.

Lisa cut her voice off in midcheer. She saw Betsy standing right next to them, and she felt bad about celebrating so loudly. Betsy had ridden well.

"Don't worry about it," Betsy said. She walked the horse she was leading into their circle. "Do you see who I'm taking care of?"

The Saddle Club girls nodded. Betsy had given Danny a much-needed bath. She shook her head in frustration. "Veronica and her father are off complaining to the show officials. She did go off course—she jumped some of the younger kids' fences and almost collided with an eight-year-old boy riding a pony. She's been eliminated from the competition, so, of course, our team has been eliminated, too."

"And she asked you to take care of Danny?" Carole held her hand under his velvety nose. Danny blew into it.

"Nope," Betsy said. "She just yanked her saddle off him and left him steaming in his stall." She looked furious. "Meg's getting started on our tack while I cool him out. Trust me, we are not cleaning Veronica's tack. But we couldn't let Danny suffer."

"Of course not," Carole said. "I'm done with Starlight; I'll help you."

"Thanks." Betsy seemed about to say something, then stopped. Finally she said, "I heard about the mud in Belle's tail. I don't know for sure that Veronica did it, but she could have. She left the tack room late last night, when Meg and I were almost asleep. I thought she was just going to the bathroom. She could have done it then."

"Thanks," Stevie said. "We were pretty sure she'd done it."

"You're welcome." Betsy shook her head. "You know, when we're not around horses, Veronica and I are pretty good friends. We have a lot of fun together at school. I almost think I'd like her better if she didn't ride."

Lisa put Prancer back in her stall and helped Stevie untack Belle. "That's pretty sad, what Betsy said," she commented. "I love the fact that you and Carole ride. How were those coops, Stevie?"

Stevie grinned. "I didn't even see them," she said. "I made sure Belle was straight to them, but I looked over the top of them. I never looked at the jumps. Then, when she was coming right up to them, I shut my eyes and grabbed her mane. Belle did just fine."

ONCE LISA HAD finished helping Stevie, she took her brushes into Prancer's stall. The mare's coat was clean and dry, but she needed to be groomed thoroughly. The next day, for the dressage test, Prancer would have to have her mane braided, and Lisa knew it wouldn't hurt her to get started on that now.

Braiding took forever, but fortunately Prancer could sleep in her braids.

Lisa hummed in quiet contentment while she worked. Prancer seemed a bit tired but happy to eat hay and have Lisa fuss over her. Lisa was so lost in her own thoughts that she jumped sideways when A.J. came into the stall and said hi.

"Sorry," he added with a grin.

"That's okay." Lisa retrieved the body brush that she'd dropped and soothed Prancer with a pat. "I was just going over our ride in my mind. I wish I could always ride like that."

"I know the feeling." A.J. picked up a soft brush and started going over Prancer's face. "I came to thank you for the dance invitation," he said, not quite looking Lisa in the face.

Lisa felt herself begin to blush. She'd forgotten all about that embarrassing moment. And surely—well, A.J. hadn't thought she liked him, had he? He was great as a friend, but Lisa didn't want him getting the wrong idea.

"Do you mind if I bring my girlfriend along?" A.J. asked.

Lisa sighed in relief. "No, that's fine," she said. "Anyone can come." It occurred to her that maybe that was why Bart had seemed so hesitant. "Tell Bart—tell him he can bring his girlfriend, too," she said, trying hard to sound indifferent about it.

A.J. laughed. "Not likely," he said. "Bart doesn't have a girlfriend. Didn't you hear what he said to you today? He really is a lot more comfortable around horses than girls."

"Oh," Lisa said. She brushed Prancer's flank carefully.

"In fact," A.J. said slowly, "you're the only girl I can think of that he really talks to at all."

"Oh," Lisa said again. She tried hard to keep her voice casual, but she was afraid she wasn't quite doing it. She could feel heat rising to her face. If only she didn't blush so easily!

Now A.J. was watching her and she was avoiding his eyes. "He's a really nice guy," he said, "and I think you'd really like him."

Lisa didn't say anything. She brushed with great concentration.

"So what I wanted to tell you is, I'll try to get him to go to the dance," A.J. said. "He doesn't usually go to dances, but with you there I'm sure he'd have a great time. So Phil and I will try to convince him. That is, if you want us to."

"Sure," Lisa said. "That would be nice. Everyone's welcome, you know."

A.J. put the brush he was using back into Lisa's grooming box. "But some people are more welcome than others," he said, laughing at her. "Don't worry,

70

Lisa. With Phil and me both working on him, how can we fail?"

After A.J. left, Lisa brushed Prancer's neck several more times before she felt her heartbeat return to anywhere near normal. She had the uncomfortable feeling that A.J. guessed exactly how she felt. Was she really being so obvious? She sighed and leaned her head against Prancer. Maybe Bart had the right idea. Maybe horses were easier to deal with than people—especially boys.

ON TUESDAY AFTERNOON Stevie breezed into the locker room just after Lisa and Carole had got there. "Guess what I saw at the Toggery!" she said. "It's a pink sweater, tunic style, with little horses appliquéd all over it!"

Carole was pulling her old riding sweatshirt over the shirt she'd worn to school. They each had a cubby in the locker room, where they usually kept their everyday riding clothes. Carole sniffed at her sweatshirt. Time she took it home for a wash. "Pink," she said, pushing her arms through the sleeves, "doesn't exactly seem like your color."

"Oh, not for me," Stevie said blithely. She yanked

open the door of her cubby and pulled out her oldest pair of jeans. She usually rode in jeans and cowboy boots rather than breeches and riding boots. "For Lisa. It'd be perfect. You know your mom would get you something new, Lisa, and besides, I bet Bart would really like it. Considering how he feels about horses and all."

Lisa blushed and threw an old sock at her friend. She'd told them about her conversations—with A.J., Phil, and Bart, and then with A.J. alone. She didn't intend to get her hopes too high. Who knew how Bart really felt? But Stevie wouldn't leave the subject alone.

"Shhh," Carole said in warning as Veronica sailed into the room. Stevie hushed instantly.

Veronica never quite looked at them. "Hmmm," she said as if to herself. "Something smells bad in here." She grabbed her leather satchel out of her cubby and stalked out the door.

"What smells bad is her attitude," Stevie remarked. "Even if Veronica hadn't managed to get herself disqualified, our team still would have beaten hers. Even if she and Danny had been perfect."

It was true. The Saddle Club had acquitted itself very well indeed. After the triumph of the cross-country rounds, the girls had ridden the dressage and show-jumping tests with confidence. Even Prancer's small blowup in the dressage ring hadn't counted too heavily against them, and when Carole got a perfect score on the written test, with Lisa close on her heels, their victory was assured.

"I don't like it," Stevie added slowly. "Veronica's being a much worse sport about this than usual. I mean, imagine, she took Danny home Saturday afternoon, even though the show officials said she could ride in the other events for practice."

"It's her pride," Lisa guessed. "She can't bear that she and Danny weren't perfect."

"That *she* wasn't perfect," Carole corrected her. "Danny had nothing to do with it. But I agree with you, Stevie. She's being a total jerk. And worse, she seems to think it's all our fault. I heard her telling Polly and Adam that. She keeps saying we made her tack fall into the mud."

"It's her guilty conscience," Stevie declared. "She played that dirty trick with the mud in Belle's tail, so she thinks everyone else would do that sort of thing, too."

Meg walked in to get ready for the lesson and Stevie hastily shut up. The Saddle Club silently finished getting dressed.

Meg looked around. "Oh, were you guys just talking about Veronica?" she asked. "Boy, is she after the three of you."

"That's totally unfair," Lisa blurted out.

"I know," Meg said. "But it's not stopping her. She's in the office right now, giving Max an earful."

Carole sighed. "She gave him one yesterday, too. I heard her."

Stevie shook her head. "At least we know Max will never believe her. Anyway, Lisa, I'm totally serious about that sweater. You've got to see it."

"Ooh, are you talking about the pink one at the Toggery?" Meg asked. "I've had my eye on it, too. It would be just perfect for the dance."

"You can have it," Lisa said. "I'm not going to get all dressed up."

"Yes, you are," Carole said, laughing. She grabbed Lisa's hand and hauled her to her feet. "You might as well face facts—Stevie and I are going to make sure you look terrific."

"Oh?" Meg inquired. "What's going on?"

"We're going to be late," Lisa said, hurrying out of the locker room. Prancer at least never bugged her.

FOR THEIR LESSON, Max saddled up, too, and rode with them out to one of the trails, where he'd built several jumps among the trees. "Now that you've all had a chance to compete this weekend," he said, "you've probably got a better idea of some of the problem spots you and your horse need to work on. So I want you to tell me what those spots are, one at a time,

75

and we'll see what we can do to make them better. Stevie?"

Stevie laughed. "Coop jumps, still. I'm not quite so afraid of them now, but I'd like to learn to jump them with my eyes open."

"Excellent," Max said. He found a hedge jump that looked very much like a coop and had them all practice it.

Carole noticed that Veronica was being ominously silent. She rode at the back of the group, stony-faced, and never said a word to Max, not even when he praised or corrected her. They worked on shadowed jumps for Betsy and jumps off a sharp turn for Meg. Lisa asked for a jump involving water. "Even though Prancer took the fence, I really had to get after her," she said. "She still hates to get her feet wet, and she pulls back when she sees water coming."

Max led them to a stream with a tiny log propped on one bank. They jumped into the water, all in a long, spread-out row. Prancer, true to Lisa's word, didn't like the water, but she followed the other horses in, and after she'd jumped the log back and forth several times, she seemed more at ease. Lisa patted her.

"Veronica," Max said sharply, "aren't you planning to jump this one?"

For the first time Lisa noticed that Veronica had

reined Danny in at the bank. "No, I'm not," Veronica said haughtily. "I don't see the point. I'd just get my breeches splashed, and it's not like Danny has any problem with water."

Danny, Lisa knew, really didn't have a problem with water. Max seemed to agree, because he ignored Veronica's tone and instead asked, "What would you like to jump, then? What problems would you like to work on?"

Veronica sniffed. "We don't have any problems. If it weren't for some people messing up our chances, we would have been perfect on Saturday."

Max's quiet voice concealed the annoyance Carole was sure he must feel. "No horse is perfect," he said, "and every rider, no matter how skilled, still has plenty to learn."

"Well, I don't want to learn anything today." Veronica seemed close to tears. Her voice was trembling. "I just can't bear to be in this lesson with people who *cheat*."

Stevie started to speak, but Max held up his hand and Stevie was still. "We'll take several jumps in order then, on our way home," he said. "Everyone keep several lengths between you and the horse in front of you, and stop if anyone has a problem. I'll bring up the rear. Go ahead, Veronica."

Stevie couldn't believe Veronica was getting off so easily. If she ever spoke to Max like that, she'd be grounded for a week. Plus, it burned Stevie up that Veronica kept calling them cheaters. She'd pointed out the dangling bridle rack to Veronica. She'd even offered to help!

They rode back quietly. As Max dismounted, he asked The Saddle Club to come to his office when they were finished taking care of their horses.

"Sure," Lisa said. Max often asked for their help with different projects. She hoped it was something exciting this time.

When they went into the office, however, Lisa could see that Max wasn't planning anything fun. With a very serious look on his face, he asked Carole to shut the door. She did. Lisa suddenly felt as if she was in trouble, but she didn't know why.

"Veronica's been saying a lot of things about you three that I don't like to hear," he began. "You know that I expect—and that the Pony Club expects—certain standards of behavior to be upheld, both here at the barn and anywhere you represent the Pony Club or Pine Hollow."

"Of course, Max," Carole said, looking confused. "But Veronica's the one who's misbehaving, not us. We're sorry about what happened to her, but we didn't have anything to do with it."

"That's not how I understand it," Max said. "I really didn't think there could be anything to her accusations—at first. I know Veronica likes to complain. But I don't think she'd persist this long if there weren't some truth to what she's saying. And in this case, any truth is too much. Did you break her bridle rack or fill her tack room with mud?"

"Max!" The three members of The Saddle Club were so astonished that they all spoke at once.

"We'd never—" Lisa said.

"I even said I'd help her—" Stevie protested.

"Max," Carole repeated, "you know us. You know we'd never do anything like that. I don't ever want to win if I can't win fairly."

Max took a deep breath. "It's not that I don't want to believe you—"

"Then believe us!" Lisa said. They told Max the whole story of the weekend—from Meg and Betsy doing all Veronica's work, to Stevie's finding mud in Belle's tail, to Stevie's offering to help Veronica. "Even after her saddle fell, we tried to help," Lisa said. "But she started yelling at us right away. I think she just feels bad about messing up—she and Danny would have been fantastic if she'd even paid attention to what Stevie said. And she doesn't want it to be her fault; she'd rather it were ours."

"Plus, she tried to wreck our chances," Stevie said. "If she blames us loudly enough for what happened to her, then maybe we won't be able to blame her for what she did."

Max shook his head. "Did any of you see Veronica

in Belle's stall?" he asked. "I don't like anyone—you or Veronica—making unfounded accusations."

"But that's what you're doing!" Stevie said. "You should consider our reputations and Veronica's, then figure out who's telling the truth."

Max shook his head but, for the first time, grinned. "Veronica's reputation is pretty tarnished, I admit. But, Stevie, so is yours. I seem to remember several incidents around the stable—"

"But not like this," Stevie said. "I want to win, all right, but I don't cheat. You know I don't. I never have."

"I know," Max admitted. "I also know how much you three dislike Veronica. And I can't help thinking that mud isn't exactly Veronica's style. I've never known her to get her hands dirty.

"So," he continued, "what I'll say is this. I won't blame you three, and I won't blame Veronica, and I won't hear another word from anyone on this subject. And nothing—*nothing*—like this had better ever happen again. No getting even, Stevie Lake. Do you hear me? This all gets dropped now."

"Of course," Carole said. She felt relieved; she could tell Max was listening to them, and she felt certain he believed them.

"I don't need revenge now," Stevie said saucily. "Why should I? We won."

Lisa swung the office door open and very nearly

walked into Veronica. "Oh—hi!" she said, startled. "I didn't know you were standing right there."

Veronica brushed past Lisa and Stevie and Carole. "Max," she said sweetly, "do you think Danny's going to need his turnout rug anymore? It's getting so warm. I could take it home and have the maid wash it."

"Whoa," Carole said as they walked toward the locker room. "That was weird. What's gotten into Max?"

"He's been worn down by two days of constant Veronica," Lisa said. "What was she doing right outside the office? I'd swear she was listening through the door."

Stevie nodded. "I thought so, too. And I didn't like the way she was smiling. She's up to something. She's not going to let this drop."

Carole shrugged. "What can she do?"

"I don't know," Stevie said, "but I bet that sooner or later we'll find out."

"REALLY? COOL!" STEVIE said into the phone. She waggled her hand at Lisa and Carole and gave a thumbs-up sign. Lisa rolled her eyes in response, but she still felt a little jolt of excitement run through her. Stevie was talking to Phil. It was Friday night, and they were just about ready to leave for the dance. "See you in a few minutes!" Stevie cooed. She hung up and grabbed Lisa's hands, spinning her around.

"He's coming!" she said. "It's official! Bart's coming to the dance! *Whee!*"

"Stop it!" Lisa said, laughing. She could feel herself starting to blush again. "I mean, I'm glad, but—

just stop it, Stevie. It's not like he's coming with *me* or anything."

"But he's coming," Stevie said practically. "That's a lot better than him not coming."

"True." Lisa grinned. "So, how do I look?" She struck a ballet pose in the middle of Stevie's bedroom. They had all decided to spend the night at Stevie's. Mr. and Mrs. Lake were going to drive them to the school and then go out to dinner and a movie with some friends before picking the girls back up.

"Fabulous!" Carole answered. Lisa hadn't bought the pink sweater that Stevie had so admired, but she had done a little shopping with her mother the evening before. She had on a brand-new pair of dark blue jeans, a white short-sleeved sweater, and a new pair of off-white sandals.

"Mom won't let me wear actual white shoes before Memorial Day," Lisa explained as she fastened her sandal strap.

Stevie nodded, though she had no idea what Lisa was talking about. Lisa's mother had very old-fashioned ideas about clothing, and it was a miracle she hadn't expected Lisa to wear a velvet dress to the dance. Stevie said so.

"Oh, no," Lisa said, laughing. "She thinks you can only wear velvet between Thanksgiving and New Year's."

Stevie shook her head. She knew she would never

understand. "What do you think of this?" she asked, zipping her skirt and holding her hands out to show off to her friends. Stevie almost never wore skirts, and when she did they were very modern, like this one—a short, straight, jazzy black knit. Stevie's sweater was pink—a shocking, electric, Stevie-like pink.

Carole laughed. "You two will put me in the shade. I'm just wearing old leggings and tennis shoes."

"Yeah," Stevie argued, "with the most fantastic top I've ever seen." Carole's shirt was a cross between a sweater and a sweatshirt. It was bright yellow, a shade that perfectly complemented Carole's skin, and it had concentric red and purple designs on it. "It's sort of a take on an old African design," Carole explained. She carefully fastened her wooden horse necklace—a very old family heirloom—around her neck, then brushed her hair back into a low ponytail. "I'm ready," she said.

"Me too," said Stevie. When Lisa nodded, Stevie said, "I'll go see if my folks are ready." She started toward the door, but before she reached it, her phone rang again.

"That's Phil," Lisa joked, "calling us to say that Bart isn't coming after all."

Stevie shook her head at Lisa. "Stevie Lake," she said cheerfully into the phone. Then, as her friends watched, the color seemed to drain out of her face. "Sure," she whispered. "But what—Sure. We'll be right there." She hung up the phone.

"That was Max," she said to her friends. "There's some sort of problem at the barn. He *says* it's not our horses, but he needs us there right away."

"It must be the horses," Carole said. They clattered down the stairs and quickly convinced Stevie's parents to take them to Pine Hollow instead of the dance.

"If we take you there, we can't come get you and take you to the dance," Mrs. Lake warned. "We've got plans tonight, for once, and we're not interrupting them to taxi you around."

"That's fine," Stevie said distractedly. She'd been looking forward to the dance for weeks, but at this moment it hardly seemed to matter at all. "I don't think we're going to the dance. Max seemed really upset. We'll just get him to drive us home whenever we're done at the stable."

"I wonder what it could be," Lisa said.

"The horses," Carole said again. "Starlight." She shivered, thinking of all that could have happened to her beloved horse. He could have colicked or foundered or cast himself in his stall . . .

"He said it wasn't the horses," Stevie said. "He wouldn't lie to us."

"What did he say exactly?" Lisa asked.

"That there was a problem at the stable, and he wanted the three of us there immediately. Then he said not to panic, it wasn't our horses, and then he hung up."

"Okay," Lisa said. She patted Carole's arm. "It'll be okay." But she didn't have the first clue what the problem could be.

When Stevie's parents pulled up at Pine Hollow, most of the stables and even Max's house were dark. Only the windows of the office and the first section of stalls were lit. In the driveway, a car sat with its engine running. The Saddle Club could see Deborah, Max's wife, and Maxi, their baby daughter, waiting inside. They waved, and Deborah waved back. The girls tumbled out of the car, and Stevie's parents left.

The girls hurried into the stable. Max was pacing up and down in his office. "Gosh," Stevie blurted, "you look really nice." Max was dressed for an evening out. He wore clean khaki pants and a nice sweater, and his hair was still damp from a shower. His expression, however, was anything but nice.

"I don't feel nice," he said. He snapped the office lights off and pointed the girls down the stable aisle. "I feel annoyed, delayed, and most of all, disappointed. Also, I admit, rather furious." He pointed toward Danny's stall.

Carole felt her mouth drop open so fast she was

surprised that it didn't hit her knees. Danny's stall was a wreck—absolutely and completely trashed. Slick, dark, half-dried mud was slathered all over the bedding, halfway up the walls, and all over poor Danny himself. His lovely gray coat was covered from nose to hoof to tail.

Stevie and Lisa were likewise stricken dumb, but Max seemed more than capable of speech. "It's just a good thing I decided to check on the horses one last time before we left," he said. "As I'm sure you know, we've had a very quiet afternoon here. In fact, you three were the only kids around. The mud's getting fairly dry, so I guess this happened around an hour ago—plenty of time for you to go home and get yourselves cleaned up."

"But Max!" Lisa protested. "We never—"

"I said I wanted these pranks stopped," he said. Lisa had never seen Max so angry. "They don't have a place in my barn. Veronica's tack looks exactly the same way. It could be ruined, for all I know. I asked my mother, and the only people she saw down here all afternoon—the *only* people—were the three of you."

The Saddle Club had taken a short trail ride that afternoon, and Stevie remembered how quiet the stables had been. But she also knew that when they left, Danny and his stall had been sparkling clean. "Veronica—" she began.

"—would have been very noticeable, pulling up in her chauffeur-driven Mercedes," Max said dryly. "I don't want to hear any theories, Stevie. I don't want to hear a word. I don't care what kind of explanations you three have. I want horse, stall, and tack *spotless* by the time I get back here. I don't care if you have to work until dawn."

He turned on his heel and started walking toward the door. The girls looked at each other in stunned silence. "But we're going to a dance," Stevie said quietly.

"No," Max said, without turning around, "you *thought* you were going to a dance. I'm afraid you have work to do." The stable door shut behind him with a click, and the girls could hear the car pulling away. They looked at each other hopelessly.

"He can't really think—" Carole said.

"He does," Stevie said. "Wow. He really thinks we did it."

"He's just so angry right now," Lisa guessed. "He might listen to us later—like, in about a week or three."

"Right. But what about tonight?"

They surveyed Danny in silent gloom. He looked truly horrible. Mud made his mane stand up in tufts like a punk rocker's hair. "Poor boy," Carole murmured, patting the one non-muddy spot on his nose. "Who would do something like this to you?"

"I guess we have to clean him up," Lisa said with some reluctance. She felt sorry for Danny, but she didn't like being blamed, even temporarily, for something she didn't and wouldn't do.

"You guess?" Stevie said. "Do you want to have Max come back and see this horse like this again? He'd kick us out of the stable forever, if he didn't kill us first."

"Plus, it's not fair to Danny," Carole said. "I don't think we have a choice."

Lisa blew out her breath. She looked at her new white sweater. "Let me go see what else I can wear," she said. Unfortunately, she'd cleaned her cubby out that afternoon, and, like her two friends, had taken most of her grubby old clothes to Stevie's house. They were in the Lakes' washing machine at this very minute.

"Oh, no," Stevie said, realizing what Lisa was thinking. "That was lousy timing, wasn't it? And I felt so virtuous, putting all that laundry into the machine."

It was true. Even combining all that they had in their three cubbies, plus everything they could drag out of the lost-and-found box, they couldn't do much to protect their party clothes. Stevie found some crusty socks and exchanged her sandals for cowboy boots, but she was still stuck in a skirt. Lisa put on a pair of Carole's old paddock boots instead of her sandals, and Carole managed to exchange her leggings for a pair of breeches, but that was all.

They had just gone back to Danny's stall when they heard the main door open. Carole's first thought was that it was Max, back already, and he was going to be furious. But it was worse than Max. It was Veronica. She was wearing an ivory satin ensemble, dance shoes, and tons of jewelry, and she flipped her lustrous hair in The Saddle Club's direction as she walked to Danny's stall.

"My," she murmured, raising an eyebrow at them, "he is a mess, isn't he? When Max phoned, I was so . . . surprised. But then, I'd been getting ready for the dance all afternoon. I took a mud bath—so good for my complexion." She grinned.

Lisa heard a strangled noise that she guessed was Stevie trying to hold her temper.

"It's such a shame that you girls won't get to come to the dance," Veronica purred. She held a carrot out to Danny, and he took it. "But then," she continued, giving The Saddle Club another glance, "I can see by the way you look that you weren't really planning on going. Stevie, those boots are adorable—and that skirt is just right for cleaning stalls."

Stevie lunged toward Veronica, but the other girl was already tripping back toward the door. "Mustn't keep the chauffeur waiting," she said. "Toodleoo.

And don't forget, I like all my tack oiled except for my saddle."

"I'll kill her," Stevie spit. They heard Veronica's car pull away. "Did you see her face? And that comment about mud baths? She set this whole thing up! She did it! I hate her!"

"We don't have a choice," Lisa said grimly. "We have to clean Danny up. Max said so."

"Oh, Max!" Stevie paced the aisle in fury. "He and Veronica are acting just alike! What was it Meg said? She felt like Cinderella? We're Cinderellas! Don't you see?"

Lisa did see, and despite the awfulness of the situation, she had to laugh. "Sure," she said. "That's us exactly. Max is the wicked stepmother, Veronica is the wicked stepsister—"

"Danny must be a toad or something—the ugly toad—"

"Wrong fairy tale," Carole cut in. "But it doesn't matter, because it all means the same thing. We can't go to the ball."

9

THE SADDLE CLUB stared glumly at Danny. The horse, looking for another carrot, nosed at them hopefully. The mud didn't seem to be bothering him, though Carole knew it could irritate his skin if it was left on him for a long time.

"Do we have to?" Stevie wailed.

Lisa slumped down onto a hay bale in the aisle. She put her chin in her hands. "There's 'have to' and 'have to,' " she said. "Nobody can force us to clean up that horse—"

"—and the stall, and the tack—"

"Right. But I think it's probably best if we do. Max looked pretty serious."

"He *can't* think that we would do something like this," Carole said, sitting down beside Lisa.

Lisa looked sideways at her friend. "Maybe he doesn't. Maybe he doesn't even care who did it. Maybe he's just sick of this stuff going on at his stable, and he wants to stop it, and he thinks this will do the trick."

"If Veronica wins here," Stevie moaned, "she'll torment us forever. Not that it matters, because as soon as I get to the dance, I am personally going to take her out."

"Which brings up another point," Lisa said. She chewed on the end of her hair, something she tended to do when upset. "How do you think we could actually get *to* the dance, if and when we're ready to go? My parents are out of town, remember? They went to see my aunt."

"And my dad's supervising weekend maneuvers at some base down in Georgia," Carole said. Her father was a colonel in the Marines.

"And my parents will kill me if we call them out of the theater," Stevie said. "We told them Max would take us home. Where's Mrs. Reg?"

Carole shook her head. "Gone. I don't know where, but if she were here, some of the lights in the house would be on."

"Maybe we could walk to the school," Stevie suggested.

"Six miles, at night, in my sandals?" Lisa said. "Besides, we'd have to cross a highway. We can walk back to Stevie's house, but we can't walk to the school."

"The highway means we can't ride there, either," said Carole. "It would be too dangerous for the horses."

"We could hitchhike."

"Stevie!" Neither Lisa nor Carole took that seriously.

Stevie sighed. "I guess we're stuck. When's Max getting back? Where did he go, anyway?"

Lisa shrugged. "I never heard him say where he was going. If they took Maxi, they can't be out that late."

"Unless they were dropping her off with Deborah's mom," Carole said. "Then they could be out all night."

"In which case, we don't have to clean the horse until morning."

"Stevie, you know we do. Besides, if we're stuck here, we might as well start working."

They got out their grooming buckets, but Danny was still a hopeless case. The mud on his body hadn't fully dried, and until it did, brushing it would only drive the dirt farther into his coat.

"We'll have to wait until he's all the way dry, then

94

whack the big clods out with stiff brushes," Carole said. "Then curry and brush him forever to get out all the dust." She groaned. Grooming was never easy when the horse had rolled in mud, and Carole had never seen an animal more thoroughly coated than Danny. Restoring him to his usual pristine state was going to take forever, even with three of them working.

"We'll start on the stall," Lisa said. "I'll put him on the cross-ties." She haltered Danny gingerly, then led him out to the aisle. Danny rubbed his head enthusiastically across Lisa's shoulder. "Oh, Danny!" Lisa cried, looking at the streak of mud running down her new white sweater. "How could you!"

"Simple," Stevie said, coming out of the stall with Danny's grimy water bucket. "Mud itches, and you looked good for a scratch."

Lisa was fighting back tears. She'd had such hopes for this night. "See how many jokes you make when it's your clothes that get ruined," she spit at Stevie.

Stevie put down the water bucket and displayed a muddy skirt. "I can never take down full buckets without leaning right against them," she said. "And, of course, I always splash water on myself."

"I'm sorry," Lisa mumbled. "It's just mud, after all. It'll wash out. Only—I keep thinking—Bart finally decided to go to the dance—"

"I know," Stevie said. "I keep wondering what Phil is going to think when I don't show up. I hope he won't be angry."

"He won't be angry at you," Carole said. She was handling a wheelbarrow very gently to try to keep her own shirt clean. "He might get worried, but he'll understand once you tell him what happened. How are we going to get the mud off the walls in here?"

Stevie and Lisa went into the stall. "Maybe brushes?" Lisa suggested. "A broom?"

"A power water hose," Stevie said.

Carole raised her eyebrows. "That would do it, but where would we get one? I guess a broom is our best bet." They started whacking at the dirt smeared on the sides of Danny's stall. The brooms did remove it pretty well, but instead of just falling to the ground, the dirt seemed to fly up into their clothes, faces, and hair. Soon they all looked as though they'd been dipped in powdered dirt. Lisa sneezed.

From the office, they could hear the phone ringing. It sounded very far away. "Just ignore that," Lisa said. "It's after hours; the answering machine will pick up." The phone stopped ringing, but after a moment it started again.

"It's Max checking up on us," Stevie decided. She ran down the aisle and caught up the receiver. "We're still here," she announced.

"What I'd like to know is what you're doing there

in the first place," Phil said. "Though when you didn't show up here at the dance, I knew you couldn't be anywhere else. Belle's not sick, is she? Are you okay?"

At the sound of his sympathetic voice, Stevie nearly dissolved. "Oh, it's so awful!" she wailed. She told him the whole story.

"That really stinks," he agreed. "I'm using the pay phone at the corner of the school, and I can see Veronica from here. She's dancing with some eighth-grader—some stylish-looking red-haired guy."

"I know him," Stevie said. "Carole and Lisa told me all about him. His name's Stone or Rock or something like that. Apparently he's new in town, and all the girls have this huge crush on him. He's rich, too. I can't believe it. Not only does she get to go to the ball, she even gets the town prince."

"What?" Phil asked.

"Never mind."

"Well, I wish I could help, but I don't see how I can, aside from pulling down the whole tent on their heads. In a few years, when I have a driver's license and a car—"

"—we should be just about finished cleaning this horse." Stevie laughed despite herself. "It's so hopeless. You have no idea."

"I'll see what I can do about the tent," Phil promised. He hung up, and Stevie trailed dispiritedly back to her friends.

"I'm glad he won't be worried about us," Carole said.

"Did Bart come?" Lisa asked.

Stevie put her hand over her mouth. "I forgot to ask. I'm sorry!"

Lisa snorted. "What difference does it make? It's not like it changes anything. I'm here, no matter where Bart is."

Half an hour passed. They decided the stall walls looked as good as they were going to look. "He'll need fresh bedding," Carole said. She grabbed the wheelbarrow again.

Lisa ran her hand along the top of Danny's back. "He's still wet. It's amazing how thick this mud is."

"Come on," Stevie said to her. "We can get started on the tack."

They went into the tack room but ran back out when they heard Carole scream, "Danny!"

"I was the only one of us who looked even halfway clean," Carole said. "Now look!" Danny had blown green horse slime across the front of her sweater. "He's ruined it!"

"If you sort of look sideways at it and squint,"

Stevie offered, "the green looks like part of the pattern."

"Oh, it does not," Carole said crossly. "This whole evening is a disaster."

"I know," Stevie said. "What we really need is a fairy godmother."

"HUH," LISA SNORTED. "A fairy godmother? I'll look in the yellow pages. Would that be under F for *fairy* or G for *godmother?*"

"Under I for *impossible*," Carole said. She dumped the wheelbarrow load of fresh shavings into Danny's stall and joined Lisa and Stevie, who had returned to the tack room. Veronica's tack wasn't quite as bad as they'd feared. Working quickly, they took the bridle apart and dunked its bit into a bucket of hot water. They got out Max's saddle soap and began cleaning the leather pieces.

"We could at least hope," Stevie persisted.

"Why?" Lisa asked. She glared at Stevie over the bucket. "Have you ever seen us in a situation more hopeless?"

"You're such a pessimist," Stevie shot back. "What we need here is a plan."

"A miracle," Lisa said. "Think one up, Stevie, and I'll go along with it." She couldn't help the angry tone she knew was in her voice. She'd been looking forward to the dance so much. She knew that it wasn't Stevie's fault they couldn't go, but she felt she had to blame *somebody*.

Stevie thought while they finished the bridle. Surely there must be something they could do. Lisa reassembled the bridle while Carole and Stevie started on the saddle. It wasn't often that Stevie Lake was stumped for a plan. In fact, Lisa couldn't remember its ever happening before. But now she seemed entirely, hopelessly, completely stumped.

"The fairy godmother is our only option," Stevie said at last. Lisa snorted. "I wish you'd quit making that noise," Stevie said.

"Sorry," Lisa said. "I'm in a bad mood, but I know it's not your fault any more than it's mine or anyone else's."

"It's Veronica's," Stevie said. There was another noise.

"Cut it out!" Stevie said. "That's so rude!"

DICKINSON AREA PUBLIC LIBRARY

"I didn't do anything!"

"There it is again!"

"It's not Lisa," Carole said. "It's something outside. Listen."

They went to the door of the tack room. From there they could make out the noise of a truck pulling slowly into the gravel driveway. Carole turned on the outdoor lights. "It's Judy!" she said. Judy Barker was Pine Hollow's veterinarian, and she was a favorite of the three girls.

The Saddle Club hurried out to greet her. Behind her heavy-duty pickup truck she was pulling a two-horse trailer—the reason, no doubt, that she was driving so slowly.

"Hey!" Judy greeted them as she got out of the cab. "I didn't expect a welcoming committee. I told Max I'd be bringing Mrs. Repass's horse back from surgery, and he told me everyone would be gone. What are you guys doing here?"

"Suffering," Stevie said succinctly.

"I can see that," Judy said, looking them over. "Those aren't exactly barn clothes you're wearing, are they? Are the horses okay?"

"They're fine," Carole said. "It's a long story."

"A horrible story," Stevie added. "Veronica stuck us here taking care of her horse while she's at the big junior-high dance."

"Max said we couldn't leave until everything was

clean," Lisa added. "We've done the stall and the tack, but Danny is going to take *hours*. He's all over crusted mud."

Judy looked confused. "You'd better tell me the whole story," she said. "I'll unload Mrs. Repass's horse. You guys talk."

They filled Judy in while she carefully backed one of the adult boarders' horses down the trailer ramp. "It's so unfair!" Lisa added as they followed Judy and the horse down the aisle of the stable.

"I'd say so," Judy agreed. "Max was upset, and unfortunately he took it out on you. You guys definitely deserve to be at that dance." She smiled. "I think you should go. In fact, I think I can fix everything."

"But that's impossible!" Lisa said.

"It's too much," Carole agreed. "Danny's such a mess. We haven't been able to get started on him yet, it's going to take hours—"

"—and none of our parents are home to take us to the school—"

"—and we can't go like this!" Stevie said, holding out her grimy shirt. "We look like we've taken baths in a pigpen!"

Judy smiled harder. Then she laughed. "Don't worry," she said. "I can easily drive you there myself, and I don't mind picking you up when it's over, either. My husband is out of town and I was planning on making a few late-night calls.

"Your clothes," she added, "are a problem. But fortunately I don't dress up very often."

The Saddle Club had never seen Judy dressed in anything more formal than a sweater and khakis, and tonight she was wearing old jeans and a sweatshirt. Stevie looked Judy over. She was about the same height as the three of them, and she wasn't very large—but surely Judy didn't mean they could trade clothes. Stevie would rather go in her own dirty shirt than in Judy's dirty shirt. Besides, there were three of them.

"Come on," Judy said, leading them back to her truck. She threw open the passenger door. "Ta-da!"

"It's a truck," Lisa said, totally confused.

Judy reached behind the seat. "It's my dry cleaning," she said. "Look, I only take it in about twice a year, and, lucky for you guys, I just picked it up today. As long as you've got pants . . ." She glanced down at Carole's torn breeches.

"We've got pants," Carole said, nodding to include Lisa. "Stevie doesn't."

"Then Stevie can have the red dress," Judy said, handing a plastic-sheathed minidress to Stevie.

Stevie peeked beneath the plastic. "Cool!" she said. "Thanks, Judy!"

"No problem. And for Carole . . . Purple? Here, take this sweater." She gave Carole a short-sleeved fine-gauge sweater. "And Lisa . . . Hmm, you wouldn't look very good in my tweed skirt. Not in my white blouse, either—too fluffy for a dance . . ."

"How about this?" Lisa asked. She pointed to a plain light blue silk blouse. It wasn't as fancy as her new sweater, but she wouldn't look like a geek in it, either. "I'd be really careful with it," she added.

"Fine," Judy said. "Now, let me see this horse." They trailed back into the barn.

"He's the worst of it," Carole warned her. "The other problems were easy compared to how Danny looks. And Max—I mean, I think we'd better make sure Danny is clean before we leave. And all that dirt isn't going to just fly out of his coat. It's going to take hours."

"So you've said," Judy said. She looked Danny over, her hands on her hips. "He's a walking disaster. No problem. I'll clean him up while you girls go to the bathroom and clean yourselves up. You've got dirt down your neck, Stevie."

"But Judy—" Carole protested. She knew Max wouldn't be satisfied with a horse that was less than totally clean.

Judy made shooing motions with her hands. "Go," she said. "I'll deal with him. Go—and be sure you wash your hands before you put on my clothes."

"See?" Stevie said as they headed for the bathroom. "I told you nothing was impossible. I *told* you all we needed was a fairy godmother."

"Yes, you told us," Carole admitted. "We just didn't believe you. And I'm still not going to believe you until that horse is clean."

Lisa started to laugh. "I never thought of Judy as a fairy godmother! What do you think she'll do, wave a magic wand over Danny?" She washed her face and hands and smoothed her hair back with her damp fingers.

"I don't particularly care, as long as it works," Stevie said. She stepped out of her soiled miniskirt and into Judy's shimmering red dress. "Look, this fits!"

"It looks fantastic," Lisa said. "Wait until Phil sees you!"

Stevie grinned. "Wait until Bart sees you!"

"Wait until Veronica sees all of us," Carole added.

"Yep," said Stevie. "We'll show her she couldn't keep us from having a good time."

"We certainly will," Lisa said. A tiny flicker of an idea started in her brain. It was crazy, but it might be funny. In fact, it might be the perfect end to this strange night. Lisa smiled to herself and adjusted the tail of Judy's blouse.

"Come," cried Stevie, "our pumpkin awaits!"

When they got back to the aisle, they couldn't

believe their eyes. Danny, on the cross-ties, was nearly clean—and Judy was waving a long stick over his body!

"What's that?" cried Carole.

Judy waved the stick at them. "It's a magic wand, of course!" When The Saddle Club looked blank, she laughed. "Surely you've noticed the parallels between your problem and Cinderella's? This is a horse vacuum, guys. Haven't you ever seen one before?"

"No," said Lisa. They came closer. Down by Judy's feet was a small square canister making a familiar vacuum-cleaner noise. A thick hose connected it to the wand in Judy's hand.

"Watch," Judy instructed in a satisfied tone. She ran the wand down the one remaining filthy spot on Danny's flank. Mud and dust disappeared, leaving only shiny gray hair. "I've always wanted one of these, but they're expensive," Judy said. "Today I finally bought one, and I've been carrying it around in my truck all day. It really works!"

"That's amazing!" Carole said. "We'll just get a brush and go over his face with it."

"No, I'll get a brush," Judy said. "You three are going to concentrate on keeping clean, at least for a few minutes." She brushed Danny's face with soft, expert strokes. "Take the vacuum back to my truck. There's a hairbrush on my seat and some lip gloss in my purse. Help yourselves. As soon as I get this horse back to his stall—your carriage awaits!"

"No," Lisa said, catching hold of Danny's lead rope as Judy unsnapped the cross-ties. "You get the vacuum, Stevie, and Carole, you get Danny's tack. He's coming to the dance with us."

"WHAT DO YOU mean?" Stevie asked. "He can't come to the dance with us! He's a horse!"

"It's an open dance," Lisa said mildly. Her little flicker of an idea had turned into pure determination: Danny was coming to the dance. "Anyone can come, provided they're invited by a junior-high student. I just invited Danny."

"But Lisa . . . ," Stevie said. Usually she was the one with the crazy ideas. This one was nuts. What would Danny do at a dance?

"They said anyone could come." Lisa held firm. "They didn't say 'any people' or 'anything but horses.' "

"I'm sure it was implied," Judy said.

"Besides, he might get upset," Carole said. "All the lights and the crowd and the noise—"

"—are no more than he'd see at a big horse show," Lisa finished. "You know he's used to that. I've never seen him act excited in any situation. And the tent will seem just like the tent stalls from the rally."

The others stared at her. Carole knew that what Lisa was saying was true. Before Veronica owned Danny, he'd been a regular on the A show circuit. He'd gone to a different horse show every week of his life. He probably wouldn't be worried at all.

"But Max said—" Carole began.

"He said we couldn't leave until the stall, tack, and horse were clean," Lisa said. "And they are. We'll take good care of Danny—you know we will. All I want to do is prove to Veronica that her horse is clean."

As Lisa's words sank in, Carole and Stevie began to grin. "I guess it is no more than Veronica deserves," Carole said.

"Certainly not," said Stevie. "In fact, it's less than she deserves, but it's not a bad start."

Judy laughed. "You three are always up to something!"

"Can we take him?" Lisa asked her. "Please?"

"I guess I don't mind," Judy said. "Max shouldn't have made you stay here—I'm sure he realizes that

110

by now—and you did make sure the horse was clean. Only promise me you'll keep him safe from the other kids. Don't do anything stupid."

"We won't," Carole promised. Lisa and Stevie nodded.

"And page me the minute he's ready to come home. Don't push him to do anything he doesn't want to do. I'll have my beeper on, and I'll come right away when you call."

"Okay," Lisa said. She clucked to Danny. "Come on, buddy. You're going to the ball."

WHEN THEY ARRIVED at the junior high, the dance was in full swing. Bright strings of lights surrounded a big, open tent on the green football field; under the tent, at least a hundred kids were dancing. A DJ played records in one corner; on the other side of the tent, folding tables and chairs gave people a place to rest.

Stevie tapped her feet to the music. "Hope Danny's got rhythm," she said. Judy pulled her rig up along the dark side of the school. She stopped, and the girls got Danny out and quickly tacked him up. Lisa grabbed his reins.

"We'll lead him in to make sure he feels calm," she said. Lisa had no doubts that he would feel calm, and, sure enough, as they approached the tent, Danny seemed no more than mildly interested. He pricked his ears in the direction of the music and walked calmly at Lisa's shoulder.

"He likes it," Carole said, watching him. "Look, Stevie. It looks like Danny's matching his footsteps to the beat of the music."

"Hey," Stevie said happily. "People are starting to see us."

As they led Danny to the side of the tent, more and more kids noticed them and stopped dancing in their tracks. "It's a horse!" someone shouted. "Look at that!" Everyone who hadn't seen them stopped and looked then. Lisa saw Veronica in the crowd, talking to the gorgeous new guy. The guy was pointing at Danny. Lisa saw Veronica toss her hair and shrug.

"Let's go over and see what she says," Stevie whispered.

Lisa led Danny closer. "Hey, Veronica," Stevie called. "Look how bright and clean he is."

They could all hear Veronica's date saying, "Who would do such a stupid thing, taking a horse to a dance? What weirdos! Horses are so strange, anyway."

"I have no idea," Veronica said, leaning on his arm.

"Hey, Veronica! Yoo-hoo!" called Stevie, waving her arm. "Look! He's clean!" Lisa stopped Danny right in front of them.

"Why are they talking to you?" the hunk asked Veronica.

Veronica shrugged. She turned her back on Danny and The Saddle Club. "Silly little girls," she sniffed. "Probably couldn't get dates, so they had to bring a horse."

The hunk looked over Veronica's shoulder at Danny. "Don't they know you?"

"Oh, sure," Veronica said loudly. "I've seen them around the barn where I ride sometimes. But they're not friends of mine."

The Saddle Club girls grinned at one another. "At least we know she won't go ballistic on us," Stevie said. Carole nodded. She was relieved that Veronica didn't seem angry that they'd taken her horse from the stable. Of course, when had Veronica ever been truly concerned about her horse?

The song had stopped but another one began. Danny nodded his head toward the speakers. "You got it, buddy," Lisa said, swinging into the saddle. "Let's dance." She rode Danny into the middle of the floor. All around her, students scattered to make room. Carole and Stevie danced on either side of Danny. Lisa tried to do something like a box step: three steps up, three steps sideways, three steps back, three steps over. Even so, she felt as if she were taking up most of the floor. No one seemed to mind. Danny really did have a sense of rhythm. As he began to understand what Lisa was asking him to do, he started moving on his own, forward, sideways, and back, matching his steps to the strong beat of the music.

"Look at that horse dance!" a boy yelled. Lisa recognized him from her social studies class, and she grinned. She spun Danny into a turn on his forehand, and the students cheered. Lisa felt great. Normally she was pretty reserved, but she'd been so angry at Veronica that she'd shed her usual inhibitions. Plus, Lisa loved acting, and dancing with Danny made her feel as if she were onstage.

"Where's Phil?" she shouted down to Stevie.

"There." Stevie pointed to a corner of the floor, where Phil, A.J., and Bart were all laughing hysterically. A girl—presumably A.J.'s girlfriend—stood with them. "I just saw them. They must have been getting something to drink when we came in." She waved the boys over, and they pushed through the ring of dancers that now encircled Lisa and the horse.

"Hey," Phil yelled above the music, "that horse looks really clean!"

Lisa grinned at him. "He was all dressed up, but he didn't have any place to go!" she shouted back. Phil gave her an appreciative thumbs-up. Lisa looked to see if Bart had come closer, but he was talking to A.J. Lisa didn't mind. She felt light and happy.

When the song ended, Lisa stopped Danny square and did a gracious dressage bow. The dance floor erupted in cheers. Danny seemed to think he was at some sort of show and that he had done well: When Lisa dismounted, he nuzzled her hand for a treat. "Beautiful boy," she praised him, rubbing his head where nearly all horses liked to be rubbed.

"Here," Stevie said, holding out her hand for the reins. "Give me a turn."

"Just a minute," Lisa said. She led Danny over to Bart, who was still next to A.J. and still laughing. "Hi," she said quickly, before her natural shyness took over again. "You said you were more comfortable with horses than girls. So I brought a horse. Want to dance?"

12

BART GRINNED, AND Lisa felt her heart beat faster. "Sure," he said. Then, to her surprise, he took the reins from her and climbed onto Danny! Lisa couldn't believe her eyes. Bart turned Danny and rode him back to the center of the dance area. Another fast song started playing.

Stevie walked up to Lisa while she was still staring in amazement. "It was supposed to be my turn."

"Trust me," Lisa said, "that didn't work out the way I planned it at all."

But in the center of the floor Bart halted Danny and looked straight at her. He tipped an imaginary riding hat to her, and then he winked. Lisa had to laugh.

"I wouldn't feel bad if I were you," Stevie declared, watching the exchange.

"I don't," Lisa assured her.

Carole was talking to A.J.'s girlfriend, Sarah, explaining just who the horse was and why they had brought him. "We'd better get out there and dance," she added. "I want us to be closest to Danny so that he won't get jostled by accident."

But it turned out the students were giving Danny a wide berth, because everyone wanted to watch the horse dance. Bart was a fantastic rider, and in a matter of minutes he had Danny doing something that looked like an electric slide: walking forward, walking back, rocking forward, rocking back, doing a set of sideways crossovers and then spinning jauntily on his forehand for the quarter-turn hop. As soon as some of the students realized what he was doing, they joined it, forming a line with Danny in the center. Danny bobbed his head; he looked completely attentive but completely relaxed. Danny had always done whatever he was asked to do, but now, for the first time, Carole realized, he looked as if he was having *fun*.

Stevie and Phil were dancing side by side, but after a while Stevie danced closer to Carole and nudged her. "Look at Veronica," she whispered. "Even the hunk's starting to get into Danny."

Carole looked and had to laugh. Veronica's date was watching Danny and clapping his hands to the music, but Veronica, evidently convinced that he didn't like horses, held her arms stiffly crossed and looked completely disdainful.

"Bart's doing a great job," Carole said, "but I hope for the next song he dances with Lisa instead of Danny."

Stevie grinned. "I can take care of that. I'll tell the DJ it's time for a slow song." She ducked through the crowd toward the DJ's station.

By the time the song ended, Stevie was back. As the crowd cheered, Bart halted Danny, waved, and dismounted. Stevie took the reins. "Now it's definitely my turn," she said. "Furthermore, this horse needs a rest."

"I need a rest, too," declared Phil. As the first few bars of a slow song began playing, Phil and Stevie led Danny to the far side of the tent, near the folding chairs. A.J. and Sarah began to dance, and one of the other eighth-grade boys asked Carole. Suddenly Lisa found herself facing Bart alone in the center of the dance floor.

He smiled at her, and she felt herself blush. Again! Lisa hoped she would someday outgrow blushing. Then, to her relief, she saw that Bart was blushing, too. Somehow this made her feel much more comfortable.

"Great dancing," she said.

"Thanks," he said. "Great horse."

"It was more than that. Somehow it looked like you really could dance."

"Well, I guess it should," Bart admitted. "My mother's been making me go to dance school since the fourth grade. No, don't laugh—She's like one of those old society types who thinks every well-bred boy and girl should still know how to waltz."

Lisa wiped her eyes. "I'm only laughing because my mother is the exact same way," she said. "Why do you think I had that horse doing the box step, anyway? Only I've been taking lessons since the third grade, not the fourth. I've been at it even longer than you."

"Well." Bart held up his hands. "Seems a shame to let all those lessons go to waste. Shall we?"

Lisa had danced slow dances before, but this was the first time she had ever danced with someone who actually knew how to dance, who didn't put his arms around her as if she were a sack of potatoes. Furthermore, and more importantly, it was the first time she'd ever slow-danced with someone she cared about. It was wonderful.

Evidently Bart thought so, too, because he looked at her and smiled softly. "I guess all those lessons were worth it after all," he said.

A few minutes later Lisa became aware that she hadn't said a word in response. "Should we be talking?" she asked.

"No," said Bart. "This is good just the way it is."

Lisa felt as if her feet were floating. She danced and was perfectly happy.

ON THE OTHER side of the floor, Stevie exchanged agonized glances with Phil. When they'd headed for the one dark part of the tent, she'd hoped that— well, was it too much to want a few minutes alone with Phil once or twice in her life? Apparently it was, because they were surrounded by students who wanted to know all about Danny.

"Is that your horse?" a girl asked Stevie.

"No, he belongs to someone from my stable," she answered. Across the way, she could see Veronica apparently arguing with her date. Veronica was waving her arms and looked as if she was shouting. Stevie grinned. She wasn't going to mention Veronica's name.

"Can we touch him?" asked another student.

"Sure," Phil said. "Pat his neck, that's what he likes best."

"How would you know?" Stevie asked in an undertone. "You don't know Danny."

"It's what all horses like best," Phil said. "Besides, you don't know Danny, either. Otherwise you would have told me what a great rock-and-roll horse he is."

Stevie grinned. She showed a swarm of eager students how they could pat Danny so that he would enjoy it rather than be annoyed by it. She answered questions about his breeding and his age.

"What's his name?" asked a boy.

"His registered name is Go for Blue," Stevie said. Danny, like all Thoroughbreds, had a fancy name from the Jockey Club registry. "But tonight we're just calling him Prince Charming."

A girl brought over a bowl of carrot sticks. "Here. One of the chaperones brought these, and no one's touching them," she said. Danny stuck his nose forward eagerly and had half the carrots eaten before Stevie could say a word.

"Thanks," she finally said. Danny raised his head and dribbled orange slime. Stevie could see Lisa dancing happily. She looked for Carole and was surprised to see that her friend was already walking toward her.

"Go have fun!" Stevie said. "We're taking good care of him."

"I just had to see for myself," Carole said. "Besides, it wasn't much fun dancing with that guy anyway. I don't know anything about him except that he likes football and thinks all horses are stupid."

"So you ditched him," Stevie guessed.

"I didn't want to dance with him after he said that!" Carole protested. "I have standards, you know. And I really did want to make sure Danny was fine. I could see you were surrounded."

"And you can see he's having a good time," Phil cut in.

"I can." Carole stroked Danny's soft nose. The music switched back to another fast song, and to their amazement, Danny started walking on his own toward the floor!

"He loves it!" Stevie said. She grinned at Carole, who had sprung into the saddle. Carole took Danny for a spin around the dance floor, and then Phil took a turn. When that song was over, the DJ played another slow one. Lisa held out her hands for the reins.

"I guess it's my turn to take him," she said.

"Forget it," Carole said. "I can see Bart looking for you. And I think Danny is getting a little bit tired." Carole knew that Danny had the energy to keep going for a long time, but she thought she could feel a slight reluctance creeping into his responses. Danny wasn't enjoying himself as much as he had been. It was time to go home. "I'm going to page Judy," Carole said. "This should be our last dance."

"Okay." Lisa didn't feel disappointed. She was amazed that they'd gotten to the dance at all, she was tickled that Danny had had fun, and she was thrilled by how much she'd enjoyed dancing with Bart. Plus, she knew she'd get to see Bart again soon—their Pony Clubs were having a joint meeting in just over a week. "We've got to be going soon," she told him as they headed back onto the dance floor. "It's past our horse's bedtime."

Carole dismounted at the edge of the tent. She loosened Danny's girth and tucked the stirrups up on his saddle. A few of her classmates came toward her, but she waved them away. "I think he's tired," she said. "If you want to see him again, you'll have to come out to Pine Hollow." She walked Danny across the parking lot and called Judy's pager from the pay phone. Then she walked Danny back to the edge of the tent. She sat on a folding chair and let him graze in the grass near her feet while the last dance ended.

"You good boy," she told him, letting her fingers run through his forelock and trailing mane. "You really were a Prince Charming. We're going to take you home now, before midnight, you know. We can't have you turning into a pumpkin."

A few more students approached, and Carole stood up to wave them away. "He's tired," she said. "We're going to take him home."

They came closer anyway. "We're with the school paper," one said. "Could we just take one picture of him?"

Carole agreed, but asked them to wait until Lisa and Stevie arrived. The dance ended, and they came over quickly.

"Here." One of the girls, who carried a camera, moved Stevie into position beside Lisa.

"We'd better hurry," Stevie said. "Now that the music's playing fast again, everybody's starting to ask where Danny is. They thought he was just sitting out the slow song."

"Let's dress him up," the second reporter suggested. "Look!" She held up a baseball hat and an enormous pair of clown's sunglasses. "Will he mind?"

Lisa looked over Danny's withers. A big group of students was heading their way. "He won't mind, but hurry!"

Just as the girl snapped the picture, they saw Judy's truck and trailer pull into the parking lot. Carole took the hat and glasses off Danny and handed them back to the girl.

"That's *my* horse!" a familiar strident voice shouted.

Stevie, Carole, and Lisa looked at each other. They didn't need to turn around to know that Veronica had finally decided to claim Danny. "Run for it!" Stevie said. Carole gathered Danny's reins and they jogged him down to the waiting trailer.

"Really, it is!" Veronica yelled. "Stevie, Carole, Lisa, stop! How dare you bring my horse out here? My expensive, beautiful horse! Bring him back!"

"Sure he's your horse," they heard a student respond. "And I'm your uncle Frankie."

"If he's your horse, why didn't you say so right away?" another student pointed out.

"Good-bye, horse!" someone cried. As Judy let down the ramp of the trailer and Carole carefully led Danny inside, a whole group of students took up the cry. "Good-bye, horse! Good-bye, Prince! Good-bye!"

"Was his name Prince?" Lisa heard someone ask.

"His name is Danny!" Veronica shouted. "He's mine, I'm telling you—mine!"

Stevie dropped the crowd a curtsy, and Lisa managed to wave at Bart before they all climbed into the cab and Judy took off.

"Fun?" Judy asked, putting the truck into gear.

"Oh, marvelous," Stevie said, sighing. "And right at the end there, Veronica started to make a fool of herself. With any luck she'll keep it up after we're gone."

13

PINE HOLLOW STABLES was as dark and quiet as it had been when they left. Lisa yawned. It had been a long, strange evening.

Judy's beeper went off as they pulled into the driveway. She parked and checked the number. "It's my husband," she said.

"We'll unload Danny while you talk," Carole offered.

"Thanks," Judy said, reaching for her cell phone. "Then, if you like, I can drive you all home."

"We're staying at Stevie's house," Lisa said. "It's not far."

They unloaded Danny under the glow of the big

outdoor light. Carole slid open the wide stable door, and Lisa walked Danny inside. Stevie reached for the switch to turn on the office light. "Let's not wake them all up," she said. Lisa and Carole nodded. There were aisle lights that shone into all the stalls, but they were almost guaranteed to wake the sleeping horses.

"I hate to say it, but I'm glad Max isn't back yet," Stevie added. "After the way he spoke to us . . ."

"I know," Carole said. "I'm not feeling very happy about him, either." The one thing about the evening that still rankled her was that Max had believed them capable of such a prank in the first place—a really unfunny prank. Sure, they'd been at war with Veronica for years, but there were limits that Carole would never cross, and anything that might hurt a horse or truly upset Max was beyond those limits.

"Maybe Max will be calmer in the morning," Lisa said. "After breakfast we can walk over and try to explain." She led Danny into his stall and began to unfasten his bridle while Carole unbuckled his girth and lifted the saddle from his back. Stevie brought him a fresh flake of hay.

"He's cool and dry," Carole reported, feeling along Danny's back. "I'll just get a brush to wipe off the saddle mark." She went out the stall door and bumped smack into somebody. Carole screamed. Lisa and Stevie flew into the aisle in alarm.

"It's me!" Max said. "Don't shoot!" To their surprise, he was laughing.

"That wasn't funny—you should have said something before sneaking up on us," Carole scolded. She could hear her heart thudding.

"I know—I'm sorry," Max said. "But I didn't realize you were still in Danny's stall until it was too late. You haven't actually been here all night, have you? And why haven't you turned on the lights?

"Judy just gave me a lecture in the parking lot," he added, before they had a chance to respond. "Something about not trusting my three best riders. But I'd already figured out for myself that I went way overboard this evening and probably blamed the wrong people for what happened."

"Probably!" Stevie said. "Max, if you still think there was any chance that we—"

Max held up his hand. "I know you didn't do it," he said. "I'm very sorry that I ever thought you did. You guys have carried out a lot of practical jokes here, especially on Veronica, but you've never done anything that hindered the running of the stable."

"Or hurt the horses," Carole said.

"Right," Max said. "How is Danny, anyway? I don't think that mud would have actually bothered him much. He probably liked getting dirty for a change." Max looked Danny over briefly. If he noticed the saddle mark on Danny's back, he didn't comment. "Did Danny and I wreck your evening?" he asked. "I hope not. You guys look pretty dressed up. Didn't you say something about a dance?"

"Danny didn't wreck anything," Lisa said, telling the truth but not the whole truth. "Our evening was great."

"Danny was a real Prince Charming," Carole added. For the first time that night, she felt completely happy. She was so glad Max wasn't angry with them. "He just made our evening more fun."

"And Max, about Veronica . . ." Stevie knew that Veronica wouldn't hesitate to tell Max the whole story of the dance. Perhaps he'd better hear it from them first.

"Don't worry about Veronica," he said. "The next time I see her, she's going to have some explaining to do. I said I wouldn't tolerate this sort of behavior in my stables, and I won't. I've got to go—Maxi woke up on the way home, and Deborah needs my help with her. Do you have a ride home? I don't want you walking in the dark."

"Judy said she'd take us," Lisa said. "We're just giving Danny a last look."

"Good night, then," Max said.

"Wow," said Stevie when he was gone. "I do feel better now."

129

"We all do," Lisa said. Carole handed her a brush, and they quickly went over Danny's sleek, clean coat.

Stevie leaned against the stall wall. "All in all, it wasn't a bad couple of weeks," she said. "We won the rally, doing some fabulous riding. We beat Veronica then, and we even got the best of her tonight. And when she whines to Max tomorrow, I don't think she's going to get any sympathy. Plus, Lisa got to know Bart a little bit."

"I still don't know him very well," Lisa said. She ran the brush over Danny's face and around his eyes. "We had a great time at the dance—it was really super—but we never really talked. I still don't know anything about him except that he loves horses, is a great rider, can dance, and doesn't say much."

"What more do you want? He sounds like the perfect guy for you," Stevie said.

Lisa laughed. "We'll see," she said. "But you're right—the dance was fantastic, as far as I'm concerned."

"As far as Danny is concerned, too," Carole said. She handed the brush to Stevie. "Get to work," she said. Stevie took the brush and went over each of Danny's legs. Carole pulled a hoof pick out of her grooming bucket and started checking Danny's feet for stones.

"I agree," Stevie said. "Danny's always been so

aloof. For a horse, he's almost stuck-up. Who would have guessed he had so much rhythm in his soul? He really enjoyed the dance."

"I bet he'd enjoy a lot of things if he had a different sort of owner," Lisa said. "Someone who really loved him." She patted Danny's soft nose. She knew that Max and Red made sure he always had the best of care, but still she felt sorry for him. What she wouldn't give for a horse of her own! She would never, ever, treat it the way Veronica treated Danny.

"Oh well," Stevie said cheerfully, "if he starts looking too depressed, we can always take him to another dance."

Carole had worked her way around to Danny's back feet. Suddenly she dropped the hoof she was holding and let out a laugh. "We'll have to call the farrier in the morning," she told them. "Prince Charming here left a shoe behind at the ball."

ABOUT THE AUTHOR

BONNIE BRYANT is the author of nearly a hundred books about horses, including The Saddle Club series, Saddle Club Super Editions, and the Pony Tails series. She has also written novels and movie novelizations under her married name, B. B. Hiller.

Ms. Bryant began writing The Saddle Club in 1986. Although she had done some riding before that, she intensified her studies then and found herself learning right along with her characters Stevie, Carole, and Lisa. She claims that they are all much better riders than she is.

Ms. Bryant was born and raised in New York City. She still lives there, in Greenwich Village, with her two sons.

Don't miss Bonnie Bryant's next exciting
Saddle Club adventure . . .

HORSEFLIES
The Saddle Club #78

School has never been one of Carole Hanson's favorite things. She isn't a bad student, but she'd much rather spend time with horses than with books—until she starts doing a research project on the Greek myth of Pegasus, the winged horse. Carole had no idea school could be this much fun.

But in her rush to learn everything she can about this wonderful flying horse, she forgets about the most important horse of all—the one right in front of her, Starlight. Can Lisa and Stevie help Carole get her priorities back in order? Or is their friend lost to the past?

Saddle Up For Fun!

Join The Saddle Club

As an official Saddle Club member you'll get:

- *Saddle Club newsletter*
- *Saddle Club membership card*
- *Saddle Club bookmark*
- *and exciting updates on everything that's happening with your favorite series.*

Bantam Doubleday Dell Books for Young Readers
Saddle Club Membership Box BK
1540 Broadway
New York, NY 10036

SKYLARK

Bantam Doubleday Dell
Books for Young Readers

Name _____

Address _____

City _____ State _____ Zip _____

Date of birth _____

Offer good while supplies last.   BFYR - 8/93